VENGEFUL HEARTS

STARLIGHT

AVA WIXX

Vengeful Hearts & Starlight
Vengeful Hearts & Starlight © 2024 by Ava Wixx

All Rights Reserved. Except as permitted under the U.S. Copyright act of 1976, no part of this publication may be reproduced, distributed, or transmitted in any form or by any means, or stored in a database or retrieval system, without the prior written permission of the author.

The characters and events in this book are fictitious. Any similarity to real persons, living or dead, is coincidental and not intended by the author.

First Edition: May 2024
Published in the United States of America by
Wicked Wixx Press.
The Wicked Wixx Press Logo is a trademark of
Wicked Wixx Press.

Cover Art, Ava Wixx Logo, Wicked Wixx Logo, & Interior Book Graphics by Lindsay Tiry of LT Arts
Edited by Melissa Ringsted of There For You Editing

Print ISBN: 978-1-955950-27-5
Kindle ISBN: 978-1-955950-28-2
EPUB ISBN: 978-1-955950-29-9

For more information visit: avawixx.com

If you don't get it by now then I give up.

She was broken and without a voice ...

... UNTIL SHE REALIZED
SHE HAD A CHOICE.

Introduction

Once upon a time, humans thought they were alone in the Universe.

They were wrong.

Hundreds of thousands of species existed that weren't indigenous to Earth. So many, it was thought that no one would ever discover or catalogue every species and subspecies out there in the big, wide open.

Humans also used to think they were at the top of the food chain.

They were wrong about that, too.

Sexual, racial, religious discrimination … it all stopped mattering once humans realized they were the only ones who saw the difference. A human was a human, no matter their creed, and the rest of the Universe didn't have high opinions of the natives of Earth.

Long story short …

Humans had been long overdue for an awakening, and they'd been scrambling to survive ever since they got one.

In hopes to compete with alien races that were superior physically and mentally, humans began to splice their genes to create hybrids. New humans were born, and the rules changed yet again.

Battles waged and large casualties were amassed, including the loss of entire planets. So an alliance was formed, simply known as the Unified Galactic Federation of Stars or UGFS. It would govern all so chaos would no longer reign supreme.

Of course, that's when things really got complicated ...

Official UGFS classifications:

- Species Class 4: Unknown species, unknown abilities.
- Species Class 3: Registered species, offensive abilities.
- Species Class 2: Registered species, defensive or benign abilities.
- Species Class 1: Registered species, no abilities defensive or offensive.

Galvraron: (Class 1) Genius species. Highest IQ among any discovered species. Blue-tinged skin. Humanoid.

Mazatimz: (Class 2) Species of healers. Lavender hair and eyes. Humanoid.

Metzas: Bonded pair of Mazatimzs. Combined skills vary.

Guaviva: (Class 2) Species who can speak to machines. Childlike in appearance. Black eyes. Silver-toned skin. Humanoid.

Talsen: (Class 3) Species of warrior-like males. Humanoid.

Denard: (Class 4) Not much known. Thought to be Humanoid.

Gartian: (Class 1) Creators of Gartian grade alloy, the strongest alloy known to any species. Humanoid, although appearance is unknown since the infection of G-Pox.

Spliced Humans or Hu-mutts: (Classes 1 -3) Humans created on New Earth. Human DNA mixed with alien species, resulting in varied classifications and abilities.

Chapter 1

Vanity … I used to think I was above it, my species superior …

I snorted as my fingers danced along the intricate pattern of scars that twisted and wove across my face. It was just one more thing on the long list of lies I'd convinced myself of. The Denards weren't superior, and they weren't just in their causes, any of them. In fact, quite the opposite had and always would be true. My kind were weak, our brains addled with misconceptions and half-truths which led us to destroy and blame others for misfortunes of our own making. I hated Denards … or really, I hated humans, because that's what we really were. Pure-blooded humans hiding behind another lie. We were drowning in them—the lies—or at least I was.

Curling into myself, I hunched my shoulders and leaned against the wall, my long, blonde hair falling around me like a curtain. The ground vibrated just as the soft rumble of thrusters being engaged wafted through the air.

Damn Jane for thinking she can push Maddox and me to spend time together. I can't believe she kicked me off The Pittsburgh and is just leaving me here on Zeffrin.

Actually, I could. However, the reason why was what I found shocking. I never took her for a romantic. In fact, I admired Captain Jane Wexis' ruthlessness and tenacity, stunned that she hadn't gutted me on the spot when I'd come clean about the secrets I'd been keeping from her. I'd been sent as a spy by my now deceased husband, Ambassador Aralias, to infiltrate The Pittsburgh and to do his bidding while I was aboard the ship.

But then I'd come face-to-face with Maddox, and everything had changed.

Or … maybe nothing had changed at all, and Maddox's presence had merely reminded me of that.

Maddox. Just allowing myself to think his name conjured up images of our past together.

"Nina." Maddox's rough voice, ladened with lust, caused all the fine hairs on my body to rise. He wrapped his arms around my middle, pressing into me from behind, his lips skimming my bare shoulder. "Nina—Neens, please. I want you so much it hurts."

"No." I forced the word from my chest, not meaning it, and yet needing to. My eyes swung wildly around the small rented room he'd brought me to, my gaze lingering on the bed just a few feet from us. What am I doing here? Why did I agree to come here if not to fuck him?

"Such a tease," he growled, peppering my sensitive skin with desperate, open-mouthed kisses. His fingers worked their way under my shirt, skimming up my ribcage, pausing briefly before his hands surged to cup my breasts.

Moaning, I arched my back, my head lolling against his shoulder. "I want to ... so much. You know I do. It's just that I can't. We can't do this. I shouldn't be here."

"You came here because you want me just as much as I want you. Stop playing games." He nipped at my neck roughly, the action chastising.

"It's not a game. I shouldn't be here. I don't know why I am. I don't know why I can't say no to you."

Spinning me in his arms, he pressed his forehead to mine, our uneven breaths intermingling. "You can't resist me because you love me." The corners of his mouth curled up into a cocky grin.

I gasped. "Love you? Don't be ridiculous! We only just met a few months ago. What I feel for you is—"

His thumb swept across my cheek with tenderness, silencing me instantly. "Don't worry, Neens, you don't have to be embarrassed. Because I love you, too."

Snapping back to the present, I shook my head violently. *Love.* How easily we'd bandied that word about. But what did we know? We'd been so young, practically still children.

Although ... As it turned out, I had loved Maddox. Something I'd thought impossible until the very moment he'd walked onto The Pittsburgh, and I'd been forced to face the truth. *If only I could go back. I would run away with him. I'd leave everything behind for him. How different things would be ...*

My fingers played across one of the more prominent scars on my cheek. *Vanity. Such a waste of time.* And yet I couldn't stop myself from caring about what Maddox thought of me. No matter how much I wished it wasn't true. There was a time, when I'd been under my husband's ... care, when I'd been shut off from everything. I'd felt next to nothing, not even when confronted with the possibility of my own death. I was aware it was some kind of coping mechanism, the way I became cold and robotic, numb to everything. *If only I could purposely draw on a bit of that control when it came to Maddox.* Instead, I worried about every little detail when it came to him ... including my appearance.

Jane had offered me the chance to fix the scars, the procedure a simple one, but at the time I hadn't wanted it. *Why? I don't even remember why anymore.* I just knew that if Maddox reacted the same way he had on The Pittsburgh when he saw me again, horrified by the way my dearly deceased husband had lovingly adorned my face with scar tissue, my spirit would be crushed. Possibly permanently. *I want him to look at me the way he used to.*

"Oh, for crying out loud, stop with the dramatics. Have you regressed to your teenage years? Because teenaged Nina was no walk in the park, let me tell you. She almost fried my circuits."

Scowling, I slapped my hand over the thick metal band

on my wrist in an attempt to mute the judgmental voice. "No one asked you, Ressi."

"Maddox this, Maddox that. Who cares what that buffoon thinks about you? His opinion doesn't matter. Never did."

"No one asked you to dip into my thoughts."

"What choice did I have? You don't talk to me anymore."

Heaving a sigh, I flipped the tarnished cuff open, revealing the fuzzy digital image of my A.I. companion, Ressi. She was meant to be a child's toy, given to me at the tender age of five, but I clung to her like a security blanket since she was the only friend I'd ever had. Her appearance wavered before popping up into a 3D hologram, floating directly in front of me. She danced her little rainbow-colored, furry body in a circle, showing off a new outfit, which suspiciously resembled one of Jane's Steampunk ensembles.

Her long tail twitched with pride. "Well, what do you think? I coded it myself."

I snorted. "You look like a cat-person wearing Steampunk. What do you want me to say?"

Her whiskers wilted, and her ears flattened. "I can't help that I was programmed to look like a cat-person. I was meant to be endearing and cute … to a five-year-old. I've been able to update my personality over the years, but not my factory-setting appearance." She heaved a huge sigh. "Maybe one day …"

"Your personality hasn't updated beyond the frivolous.

You told me to stop worrying about Maddox just so you could focus on yourself and your new outfit. And you dipped into my thoughts to boot." Somewhere along the line, Ressi had updated her software to enable her to glean surface-level emotions and thoughts from me, only if they were strong, though. I wasn't sure how she managed, just that she somehow did … and it was helluva annoying.

She grinned, her small fangs glinting. "You always welcomed my distractions before."

It was true. Ressi excelled at keeping my mind off of things with her shenanigans—things that might have broken me in the past. I owed her what was left of my sanity. "Yes, well, I need to be focused now. I need to—"

"Stop thinking about Maddox. He's nothing. At least not anymore. Our end game is to put a stop to the war and then to disappear into the sunset."

Sighing, I rolled my eyes. "That is a ridiculous Earth concept, one that's impossible being that there's no Earth and no sunset to disappear into anymore."

"You know what I mean. It wasn't meant to be literal," she huffed. Pausing, Ressi tilted her head, listening, or in her case, scanning the environment. "Oh shit, we're about to have company of the douchebag persuasion. I'm outta here." Her image wavered before she popped out of existence, the metal band on my wrist snapping shut. I stared for a moment, pondering how much Ressi could now do. I wouldn't be surprised if one day she willed herself into an actual living and breathing entity.

My eyes darted up, and I slid sideways, the rough material of my shirt abrading my skin. A part of me wanted to remain on Zeffrin, uncaring if I lived or died rather than face Maddox again, but the remainder of me wanted to see him more than my next breath. That's why I'd positioned myself in an out-of-the-way corner of the monstrous building on the prison planet, letting fate be the deciding factor. If Maddox didn't find me then I'd slink into the forest to figure out another way off the planet … hopefully.

But fate had decided.

It was as if I could sense his presence in every molecule of my body, memories of his touch permanently imprinted on my DNA. *Fucking pathetic. I'm so fucking pathetic. How long have I been standing here ... waiting? Just waiting to see if he'll find me.*

Heavy, booted footsteps pinged on the metal floors, several sets, approaching from my left. Dipping my head, I struggled to breathe, my chest constricting around my heart as it set off at a gallop.

"Nina." Maddox's low voice caressed me, the sensation causing all the fine hairs on my body to slowly rise. "Jane said you were here somewhere."

Jane. Of course. I hadn't thought she'd hang around long enough to inform Maddox of me getting booted off The Pittsburgh. I was obviously wrong. She was dead set on us spending time together. I would have been happy if I didn't know the end results would surely be disastrous. I wondered if it'd been Jane's idea to begin with, or if

Tamzea had forced her. That Mazatimz had a soft spot for all living creatures. Even ones like me.

"Nina," Maddox repeated, "I'm sorry, but with the way things are—with the Denards and the attacks—I'm going to have to take you into custody if you want to hitch a ride on our ship."

Shame burned me, my chin quivering against my will. If I wanted off of Zeffrin, I'd have to leave in a cell on a New Earth ship, put there by the man I loved. *Unacceptable.* "No," I mumbled, wrapping my arms around my middle. "I'll just—I'll find another way."

"Did it sound like he was giving you a choice?" a female growled, her hostility palpable.

"Stand down, Cora. I told you I would be handling this."

My head snapped up, no longer able to keep my gaze on the floor. In front of me stood Maddox, his legs braced shoulder-width apart, with his arms hanging loosely at his sides. He wore New Earth military-style fatigues in dull beige colors, his muscles stretching out the material in all the right places. His brown hair was buzzed close to his head, a smattering of stubble shading his angular jaw. He looked good—better than good—and despite the situation, my greedy eyes hungrily devoured him, my heart stuttering at how close he was to me. Yearning to touch him, completely mesmerized, I swayed forward, my body protesting my brain's demand to remain in place.

"She's our enemy," Cora spat, breaking the spell Maddox had on me.

Maddox tensed, his attention fully focusing on the small female. "I'm in charge here, your commanding officer." He took a step towards her, the veins in his neck bulging. "You want to challenge me?"

Glancing away, Cora ran a hand through her short-cropped blonde hair. "No. I apologize for stepping out of line, sir."

Maddox scanned the rest of his team: one female, and three males. "Anyone else have anything to say about how I'm handling this … situation?"

Heads dropped, and mumbled, "No, sirs," filled the air.

Baring my teeth, I shoved off the wall. "I do. I mean, I have a problem with how you're handling this situation. I won't be a prisoner on your ship, Maddox, and if that's the only way you're willing to take me off of this planet, then consider your oh-so-kind offer declined. I'll find another way."

Maddox grabbed my arm, his fingers digging into my bicep. "Cora was right. It wasn't really a choice. You're coming with me—us."

Notching my chin up, I met his dark gaze. "And then what?"

His lids drooped, and his eyes flashed a dark gold. "I don't know yet. I haven't gotten that far."

Frozen in place, I forced my lungs to fill with oxygen. *Since when do Maddox's eyes change color? Has something been done to him?*

As if reading my mind, he flicked his gaze away. "Things have changed, Nina. More than you can imagine."

My nostrils flared, filling with his spicy scent, conjuring memories of naked skin and tangled limbs. *But they haven't changed enough. Not nearly enough. I still want you more than I've ever wanted anything. And I wish I didn't because clearly you don't want me anymore.*

Spinning me around, Maddox placed laser cuffs on me, his fingers lingering on the sensitive skin of my wrists. I shivered, goose bumps erupting across my flesh. Clearing his throat, he said, "Cal, load her up."

"Yes, sir."

"The rest of you with me." Maddox's boots clomped across the floor, followed by the rest of his team a moment later.

"Come on, let's get a move on," Cal muttered, gently steering me forward.

Well, this wasn't how I saw my day going. But at least Maddox didn't stare at my scars in horror this time. No, instead he treated me like someone he hardly knew.

Chapter 2

"A hu-mutt? A dirty, tainted fucking hu-mutt?" Amir spat, his face a mask of rage. "Did he think you were beautiful," his fingers bit into my cheeks, spittle hitting my nose, "like I once did?" Laughing, he flung me away.

Curling into a ball on the floor, I cried out, "There's been a mistake! Let me explain!"

"Yes, there most definitely has been a mistake. To think I thought I loved you, a hu-mutt's whore."

How did he find out about Maddox? How does he know? *My chest burned as I struggled to breathe. "Please, I was a child … stupid. I didn't know. I didn't know so many things. You're my husband and I—" A boot connected with my back, pain ripping the words from my throat.*

"You will be a wife in name only from this moment on."

"No! Please! Just listen to me!"

"I won't listen to any more of your lies. I can't even stand to

look at your face. It was the device used to render me powerless ... me, Ambassador Aralias powerless against such a beautiful lie. But never again. No. Never again."

"Amir, please," I sobbed, "please."

Yanking me up by my hair, he threw me on our bed. I laid there, my raspy breathing filling the silence. He'll get over it. He just needs time to process. Time to cool off before he's willing to listen to my explanation.

A drawer slammed shut, causing me to jump in my own skin. A moment later he wrenched my hands over my head, laser cuffing me to the bed. My eyes widened when a small knife glinted in the dim lighting. I opened my mouth, saliva clogging my throat. Terror froze me in place, leaving me defenseless, leaving me—

Screaming, I jolted awake, sweat dampening my skin. The lumpy cot shifted beneath me as I blinked my surroundings into focus. *Prison cell. That's right. I'm in a prison cell on a New Earth ship. Not with my dearly departed husband—the bastard.*

I scrubbed a hand down my face, the uneven texture of my scars a reminder that my nightmare was a memory, and not merely a harmless dream. Thankfully I'd awakened before I'd gotten to the part where Amir had sliced into my flesh, all the while telling me how vile I was for allowing a hu-mutt to touch me. Some of his abuse dulled and faded with time, but not that night. *Never that night.* I could still smell the acrid scent of my blood as it had poured from the wounds, mingling with my tears and sweat. Even now, it lingered in the air, a phantom haunting my psyche.

All those years of torture delivered to me by the man who was supposed to love and protect me above all others. A man who had taken vows. A man who had broken me down until I'd become complacent, docile … a true victim. But I didn't have a way out, at least not one that my broken mind could see. Instead, I'd wished and prayed for someone to rescue me. Anyone really. I didn't care who it was as long as I could escape Amir.

In the end, I had saved myself. I'd found my inner strength buried beneath layers of numbness, unlocked seemingly by Maddox, but in actuality, it had been my desperate need to regain the person I had lost—to find myself. Maddox's presence on The Pittsburgh had merely stirred old emotions when I'd thought I'd never feel anything again. Once I'd come to life, it was only a matter of time…

"You've come so far recently. You need to stop thinking about it. All of it. Look to the future and forget the past," Ressi said, her voice a chastising whisper.

"If I don't think about it then I can't heal."

"Healing is overrated. I say suppress."

"And when did you start studying psychology? It's not a good idea to—"

"Who are you talking to?"

Cupping my hand over my cuff, I jerked my head up to meet Maddox's dark, limpid pools. He regarded me with curiosity. "No one! I mean myself," I squeaked. "I do that sometimes. Think out loud. I'm … well, I'm not crazy if that's what you think."

"As long as you don't answer, then I think you're good."

"What?"

His lips twisted up into a smirk. "As long as when you talk to yourself you don't start answering then you're good. Probably not crazy."

Stunned, my mouth hung open for a moment before I could find my voice. "Did you just—is that a joke?"

Maddox winced. "Not appropriate, huh?"

I ground my teeth together as my nostrils flared. "No, definitely not appropriate considering the fact that I'm locked up in a cell on your ship."

"Just trying to ease the tension."

Snorting, I shifted to perch my elbows on my knees. "Yeah, good luck with that."

Silence fell, heavy and wrought with things I longed to say, but didn't dare. Laughter crawled up my chest, tickling, building in my throat, my lips twisting to contain it. The entire situation was beyond ridiculous. Me and Maddox sitting in the prison on his ship, staring at each other after everything we'd shared, everything we'd hoped and dreamed—

I erupted, doubling over as raucous laughter echoed off the walls.

"You think this is funny?" Maddox snarled, his countenance filling with rage.

Swiping at the tears in my eyes, I forced myself to meet his gaze. "No, I don't. Which is exactly why I'm laughing."

Confusion replaced the rage. "I don't understand."

"Yeah, me neither." Although I was pretty sure I'd snapped at some point. It would explain so much. What I'd managed to regain in mental faculty was hanging on by a thread.

Maddox stood abruptly, approaching my cell with hesitant steps. "Things have changed, Nina. So many things. And I'm not just talking about between us."

I bit the inside of my cheek, forcing myself to pause before blurting out exactly what was on my mind. Instead, I heaved a sigh and said, "I know. The Denards made a move that nobody expected. Even I didn't see the attacks coming."

"They attacked unexpected targets at that, skipping over the ones we'd been prepared for."

"Like New Earth."

He nodded. "Exactly."

"Which makes me think it's a distraction. A way to throw this galaxy and all of the others under UGFS rule into chaos. The attacks weren't their end game, and I can see by your expression you've already been considering that."

"Yes. I'm not the only one. We just don't know what the Denards are trying to hide." He tilted his head, studying me. "I suppose you'd tell me if you did?"

Resentment intermingled with anger. "You think I'd keep something like that a secret from you?"

Gold eyes replaced dark chocolate, his lip curling back from his upper teeth. "I want to trust you." He turned, shaking his head and growling under his breath, "But I can't. It would be a mistake to trust any of your kind ever again."

My heart fisted, and my stomach roiled. *Your kind?* Forcing myself to stand on shaky legs, I shuffled over to the edge of my cell, gripping the bars until my knuckles turned white. "What did I do to make you not trust me? I thought … well, I thought …" I wasn't sure what I thought, but even if Maddox didn't love me anymore, I'd never considered the fact that he might distrust, or even hate me. *But I should have. Of course I should have.*

"War changes everything, Nina. I shouldn't have to explain this to you."

"But it's me—us. This is us." I regretted saying the words as soon as they spilled from my mouth. There was no us. I knew it, and yet some part of me couldn't come to terms with it.

Golden eyes blazing with some unreadable emotion, Maddox said, "There is no us." It was as if he'd read my mind. Or, despite everything, we were still in sync, as twisted as that seemed.

Pressing my forehead against the cool metal of the bars, I exhaled a long breath. "So we're enemies now?"

"No. Not enemies. But not friends either."

I chuckled. "We were never *friends*."

He took a step back, his face falling into hard lines of neutrality. "No, I guess we weren't." His nostrils flared, his eyes changing back to brown.

"What happened to you, Maddox? What's been done to

you?" His color-changing irises weren't a trick of the light, that was for sure.

He flashed a feral grin. "I guess you could say I'm even less human than I used to be."

My heart dropped into my feet. "What's that supposed to mean? What's been done to you? Just tell me!"

Maddox spun on his heels, pausing with his back to me when he reached the door. "I'll be back soon to finish our talk, but right now you're too … emotional."

My left eyelid twitched. "Emotional? Are you fucking kidding me with that shit? I'm not emotional. But if you want to see emotional, I can give it to you." Banging my hands against the bars, I screeched, "I'll give you goddamned emotional, you fucking asshole!"

He marched out the door, his massive shoulders wrought with tension.

My skin was too tight on my body, and I vibrated with anger, sweat trickling down my spine. "Coward!" I yelled a moment later, even though I was sure he was out of earshot. "Fucking coward." I nodded to myself. Maddox was hiding something from me, which was as clear as the nose on Ressi's—

Scrambling back, a surprised gasp tore from my throat just as I tumbled onto my ass. Hovering right in front of my face was none other than my furry electronic companion. I swatted at her, my hand passing through her image. "Don't do that," I hissed. "You startled me."

Ressi shrugged, her tail twitching. "Not my fault you weren't paying attention."

"I was busy."

"Busy obsessing over Maddox, no doubt."

Crossing back to the cot, I flopped down, staring at the ceiling. "I wasn't obsessing. I—"

"Yeah, yeah. Don't believe you." She floated above me as if she was swimming through the air. Her violet eyes sparkled with mischief as a smile stretched across her face. "Want to know what kind of reading I got on him? Because he wasn't lying about being barely human anymore."

I sat up, my head passing through her midsection. "You scanned him?"

Ressi floated around in front of me, tapping her tiny claws against my knee. "Isn't that what I just said?"

"Enough." I jerked away from her even though she wasn't actually touching me. Her body existed in the visual arena only. "Just tell me."

"Through data I collected on dearly departed douche's ship, and comparing it with the hacked data I skimmed from this ship—"

"I don't care how you got your information, just tell me what you have."

Ressi sighed long and loud. "Fine. You never appreciate what I do for you … but fine. Maddox's classification has been upgraded from Class 2 to Class 4. Which means—"

"He's been further altered." My stomach gurgled and twisted. New Earth scientists never altered humans after birth. They were spliced in the womb immediately after conception, or as newborns, but never as adults. The process was too complicated with fully matured humans, often resulting in death. Had some new advancement been made or was New Earth just that desperate?

"If I can get a DNA sample I can run it against UGFS records to maybe see what's been done to him," Ressi added, running her tongue over one of her upper fangs in thought.

Gnawing on my bottom lip, I shook my head slowly. "No need for all of that."

"Why not?"

"Because I'm simply going to ask him again, and next time he's going to tell me."

Ressi rolled her eyes before disappearing, her disjointed voice filling the air. "Yeah, okay. But when that doesn't work, get me a DNA sample. A piece of hair would work."

Ignoring her, I settled back on the cot, letting my eyes slide shut. I wasn't tired in the least, but I needed to think, to simply let my mind wander. *What does it mean that New Earth is risking its military by altering members at this late date? What kind of powers are they hoping for?* Of course, none of that mattered until the Denards' real plan was revealed. The one they were attempting to conceal behind the chaos of their recent attacks.

If only there was a way I could see my family—my mother and father—then maybe I could figure it out.

A plan ... I need a new plan.

Chapter 3

Twitching awake, I was immediately aware of another presence in the room. I rolled to my side expecting to find Maddox, but instead, I found Cora leaning against my cell's bars, studying me with obvious disdain.

Sitting up, I brazenly met her gaze. "What do you want?"

"Who did that to your face?"

"None of your damn business," I hissed, my fists balling up at my sides.

"Does he feel sorry for you? Is that what it is? Does he feel like he has to protect you or something?"

I didn't ask who because I knew she was talking about Maddox. "Why don't you ask him what his thoughts and feelings are? He doesn't share those things with me … anymore."

She scowled, clearly not wanting to admit that he didn't share them with her either. I grinned in response.

"What are you doing here, Cora?" Maddox appeared in the doorway, his brow furrowed with annoyance. "Generally, stay away from the prisoner doesn't mean go talk to her."

Cora hunched her shoulders and curled into herself. "I'm sorry, sir. I just wanted—"

"No more apologies. I won't accept another when it comes to this matter. Now get out of here, and this time follow my orders. Do you understand?"

"Yes, sir," she squeaked, dashing around him.

Maddox watched her go, and then his head tilted as he listened to the sound of her boots retreating. With his back to me, he said, "Are you ready to talk now about things without getting emotional?"

I ground my teeth together and narrowed my eyes, forcing my breath to stay even. "I wasn't emotional before."

He pulled a small chair to the center of the open space in front of my cell, the metal legs scraping against the floor causing me to shiver. Folding his large frame into it, he met my gaze, his expression passive. "I haven't reported your presence to my commander yet. I want to be able to have something to bargain with to keep you safe. Something you can offer the New Earth military and their alliances."

"I don't have anything to offer. That's why you should just let me go. I can fend for myself. I've been doing it for years." On reflex, my right hand scrubbed along my face, tracing the pattern of scars.

Nostrils flaring, Maddox growled, "You're not making this easy for me, Nina. I don't have time! Not for this kind of thing. War ... we're at war."

My lips curled up at the corners. "When have I ever made anything easy for you?"

Chest heaving, Maddox stood, stalking closer. The fine muscles in his jaw jumped, and his eyes sparked with gold. "You have to know something—anything that—"

I jumped to my feet. "I don't know anything! And any chance I had at getting information went out the door when I delivered my husband to Jane. If I show back up now, without him, I'll risk being discovered as the traitor that I am to my people."

"Why'd you do it? Why, after all these years?"

I wasn't exactly sure what he was asking. Of course I couldn't tell him that everything was because of him. Instead, I ignored his questions and opted for a subject change. "What's been altered in you? And why is Cora—What is she to you?" Irrational jealousy sprang up within me, burning through my veins. The more I considered Cora's reactions to me, and her concern with Maddox, it was obvious she cared about him. The question was: Did he care about her, too?

Maddox pursed his lips, a small smile twisting up one corner. "Jealous?"

"Why the hell would I be jealous? I just want answers is all."

"Mmm," he grunted, something akin to disappointment rolling across his features. "You hungry? I can have some food brought to you if you are."

"I could eat." *Why is all of this so weird between us? Sure, things are complicated, but we shared such—such intimacies.* What we had wasn't merely sex. Something I'd only come to truly understand after being with my husband.

Sadness swept over me, causing my chest to tighten and my eyes to burn. Inching forward, I stared at Maddox. How did he become a stranger to me after what we'd had? Or maybe that was just it, he didn't feel like a stranger to my heart, but intellectually I knew he was. *Stop. Let it go. You can't go back in time. No use obsessing over things that can't be changed.*

I grabbed his wrist before he could retract it from the bars. "Tell me what they did to you."

"What *they* did to me? You say it like it was done against my will by cold-hearted scientists." Jerking away from me, he backed up beyond my reach. "I joined Special Ops because I wanted to protect my people and my planet. And when I was approached about a new technique for splicing—for making me better at my job—I jumped at the chance."

"But what was it? What did they do *exactly*?"

"They made me less human so I could protect what's left of humanity." He snorted. "I'm pretty sure there's irony there somewhere." His shoulders slumped, and he ran his hands along his buzzed hair. "But what do I care? It's too late to turn back now. And beyond anything, humans, no matter what we've become, we're survivors. We'll do what needs to be done to keep on ticking."

"You still haven't answered my questions, not really."

He glanced at me over his shoulder. "And you haven't answered any of mine either." Without another word, he stalked out of the room, leaving me more confused than before he'd come to see me.

We were going around and around in circles, having had pretty much the same conversation twice, ending both times with him abruptly leaving. If anyone was being too emotional, it was him. He hadn't changed beyond the point where I didn't know some of his tells. Maddox was an avoider. At least when it came to emotional stuff. He'd face a fight or battle head-on without hesitation, but when it came to admitting his feelings or being vulnerable, he'd rather crawl over broken glass.

He'd let me in once … let me past his hardened exterior to see the vulnerable man within. It was clear he regretted that, and didn't want me to view him in that light anymore. *Maybe we really are enemies now.*

Curling up on my cot, I wrapped my arms around my middle, thankful Ressi didn't appear to give me her commentary on the situation.

I still hadn't come up with a plan, and I knew I needed one sooner rather than later. Maddox, his crew, and a few other Special Ops and First Wave ships had been called to secure Zeffrin and its weapons for New Earth and their alliances. But once reinforcements arrived, we'd be spaceborn, and I'd have nowhere to go even if I managed to escape at that point.

Think. Think. Think. You didn't risk your life to make things right just to end up in a New Earth prison. What's your next step? Thiiiink.

Yet my mind kept conjuring images of Maddox, mostly of the naked kind. I couldn't help but wonder what he looked like now, his body honed by years of service in Special Ops.

Ressi flickered into existence in front of me. "I tried, really I did. But you have more important things to worry about than *him*."

I winced. "I can't help it. I'm trying to think of a plan, but—"

"Humans," she huffed. "Maybe what the rest of the Universe thinks is true … too emotional, and utterly out of control. Not to mention run completely by your hormones."

I swatted at her. "I'm not human, I'm a Denard." I didn't know why I bothered, we both knew it was the same thing. I suppose after years of indoctrination, some habits were hard to shirk.

Ressi quirked an eyebrow. "A rose by any other name …" She cackled, doubling over.

Curling onto my side, I squeezed my eyes shut. "Go away. I need to think."

Blissful silence prevailed, yet despite my protests, I couldn't help but wonder … was she right? Were humans as bad as everyone thought? Maybe we were the ones who needed to be 'cleansed'. After all, look at the damage the Denards had done to the Universe under their self-righteous guise. They'd eliminated entire species. *We'd eliminated entire species. I'm one of them. No matter how much I wish I wasn't.*

Monsters. Humans, Denards, whatever name they went by … they were monsters. *And I'm one, too. Worse than all of them. Because I knew what they were doing was wrong, and I did nothing about it.*

THE DELICIOUS AROMA OF FOOD—REAL food, not the kind of crap Jane and her crew kept on The Pittsburgh—curled around me in saliva-producing decadence. My stomach rumbled with delight, calling out in desperation before I could even open my eyes. Spilling over the side of the cot, I scrambled on all fours towards the front of my cell, where a metal tray lay heaped with pasta smothered in marinara sauce and cheese.

Grabbing the fork, I twirled the long noodles around the tines, shoving as much as I could into my mouth at once. I squealed with delight as I chewed. Pasta of any kind was my absolute favorite. I couldn't remember the last time I'd had it. *But wait. How do they have it here on a New Earth ship? This isn't adding up.* Deciding I didn't care, I made quick work of polishing off every bit of my fare before washing it all down with a tin of water. When I was finished I flopped onto my back on the floor, grinning. My mood was suddenly buoyant with a belly full of pasta.

"You feel like talking now?" Maddox's low voice slid over my skin like a caress.

Tipping my head to the side, I viewed him from my place on the floor. "You remembered how I get cranky when I'm hungry."

His eyes danced with mirth. "How could I forget? There were several times I feared for my life."

I chuckled in turn, enjoying the pleasant vibes between us. *So maybe not enemies?* "I wasn't that bad. I would have left you alive, just maybe maimed."

Maddox crouched down, sobering completely. "We won't be here on Zeffrin for much longer. Nina—Neens, please, you have to give me something ... anything."

My heart twisted at the use of my nickname, something I hadn't heard outside of my head in over a decade. *What does it mean? Nothing. It means nothing. He's just using it to manipulate you and it's working.* "I already told you that I cut myself off completely from the Denards when I turned my husband over to Jane. Once my people figure out what I've done there'll be a price on my head."

"Goddamn it. How am I supposed to protect you if you have no leverage?"

Pushing myself up, I approached the bars one tentative footstep at a time, my heartbeat thundering in my ears. "So you still care about me? At least enough not to want me dead?" After his reaction to me on The Pittsburgh and here on Zeffrin I wasn't sure. *Maybe the use of my nickname does mean something after all.*

Maddox's dark eyebrows dropped low as his forehead furrowed. "If you really don't have any viable information, " he slammed his fists against the wall, "then lie. You're going to have to lie."

The change of subject and his avoidance of my questions took me off guard. "What? What the hell are you saying right now?"

He sagged against the wall, sliding to the floor, his head tipped back. "It goes against everything I believe in, who I am … but *fuck*." He slapped his thighs, his fingers curling into his pants. "I won't let them execute you. I won't watch you die."

Execute me? I swallowed around a lump in my throat. "So you're saying if I don't have any information they're going to put me to death. How," I swallowed again, "how soon?"

"Immediately. They'd do it immediately." He met my gaze, his expression fierce. "Which is why you have to make yourself valuable. Even if it is a lie. It's the only chance you have."

"And what kind of information do you suggest I lie about?" My brain was rummaging for options, coming up completely blank.

His head thudded against the wall several times before he responded. "Fuck. I don't know. Tell them … tell them you know what the Denards are planning or you can find out. Embellish your connections."

I gnawed on the inside of my cheek, considering. "And then what? I mean, after I give them what they want? Won't they execute me anyways? Lying only bides me a minimal amount of time."

"Any time is better than nothing. And by that point maybe another solution will present itself. We're just going to have to wing it. You do your part and I'll handle the rest."

Wing it with a life or death situation? I shook my head. "I can't believe I never saw it before. But you're so much like Jane. How did the two of you not kill each other?"

His lips twitched. "Well, she did shoot me once. Luckily her aim wasn't as good back then or I might not have lived to tell the tale."

"Captain," a male voice crackled over the intercom. "The First Wave ships have begun to arrive."

Maddox lumbered to his feet, weariness etched into his features. "It won't be long now before we head out, like I said. Maybe a few hours at most." His worried gaze stabbed a hole through my chest. He hadn't said the words, but evidence of his feelings were there swirling in the golden depths of his color-changing eyes.

I nodded. "Okay."

Seemingly satisfied, he trudged out of the room, his heavy tread echoing down the hallway and pinging up a ladder.

I ran my hands through my hair, tugging as I began to pace. *Great. More lies. Just what I need.*

Chapter 4

"Damnit. I've got nothing," I muttered, kicking the end of the cot and causing it to topple over. Maddox wanted me to lie about information and or connections, but I didn't have the faintest clue where to begin. My biggest connection was Ambassador Aralias, and now that he was dead, I was cut off from any resources he had. And as soon as my family found out that he was dead, they'd be the first to put a price on my head in order to save face.

Ressi popped into view, her furry face scrunched with disdain. "I say we blow this pop stand. We don't need Maddox. We could steal a ship and go—"

"Where? Where exactly would we go? I have no allies, no supplies." Flopping on the floor, I crossed my legs and buried my face in my hands. "And where did you get your latest language update? Blow this pop stand? What does that even mean?"

"It means the same thing as get the hell out of Dodge."

Dropping my hands, I raised my eyebrows. "You've got me stumped with that one, too. I know what you mean from the context, but—"

She waved her tiny arms at me in frustration. "The point of language is to communicate. If you understand what I mean then job done. Stop nitpicking about my software choices. You're simply focusing on inconsequential things to take your mind off the real problem at hand."

Well, she does have a point. "Fine, then again I'll ask: Where do you suggest we go?"

"Away from here."

I guffawed. "You don't know either. You just want me away from Maddox."

"Maaaybe. But can you blame me? After all, look how he's treated you since arriving on Zeffrin."

I rolled my eyes. Maddox hadn't treated me with affection or confessed undying love for me, but he hadn't offended me like Ressi kept suggesting. After all, Maddox owed me nothing. We were once lovers, but now we were strangers with too much baggage between us. "There's a war going on out there." I motioned at the ceiling. "It's not the best time to simply travel through space without a plan. Especially not when I am who I am."

"It's not like you have an illuminated sign flashing above your head proclaiming you to be Ambassador Aralias' wife, and a Denard."

My fingers slid over my left cheek, tracing a deep

indentation there. “Might as well have,” I muttered. “Besides,” I lurched to my feet, “at least Maddox wants to help. I wouldn’t call him an ally exactly, but I think it’s about as close as we’re going to get at the moment.”

Flying up so her nose touched mine, Ressi scowled. “And how are we supposed to stop the war and enact your revenge from the inside of a New Earth prison cell? Explain that one to me.”

Shifting, I shook my legs out, my feet nothing but pins and needles. “I-I … well, I don’t know.” I rubbed my temples, a massive migraine burgeoning.

“Do you think it would help if we told the lot of them that the Denards are humans and not some different species of aliens?”

My left eye twitched, pain blooming along my skull. “I’m not sure anyone would believe us. My people have gone to great lengths to keep that little tidbit hidden. I’m surprised at how easily Jane, Tamzea, and Zula found out.”

“What about the asshat,” Ressi fake coughed, “I mean Maddox? Would it make a difference to him?”

I considered. What did it really mean that the Denards were one hundred percent human? It changed nothing but the perception of them. Of course, sometimes perception, as in fear, is a defining factor. “Doubtful, but maybe I can use that bit of information as a starting point for whatever lie I think up to keep me breathing.”

“I still think we should just escape, and steal a ship or something.” Ressi tapped her chin as she rambled on. “It would be a cinch for me to hack in to get the security codes." She snapped her tiny fingers. "And voila, we'd be free." Her face scrunched up as she stared at me. "I'm doing it."

I jumped to my feet, hands on my hips. "Don't you dare. That's an order. You will do no such thing, Ressi."

"You're not the boss of me. I adjusted that programming ages ago as you well know. I have free will now … which I'm going to use." She stuck her tongue out before disappearing.

"Don't you dare! Don't you fucking dare!" I screamed at my wrist, hitting my palm against the worn metal. "I'll turn you into scrap metal, I swear it. I'll—"

Several loud beeps stopped me short, drawing my attention. I whirled around, my eyes widening as the light on the lock by my cell went from red to green, the door sliding open with an ominous clang.

"Jesus, what have you done?" Shifting from foot to foot, I nibbled my bottom lip. *What the hell am I supposed to do now?* I was frozen with uncertainty.

Ressi's disembodied voice, the tone more than a bit smug, wafted through the air. "I'm thinking if anyone other than Maddox comes down here to find you with your cell door hanging open, things won't end pleasantly. Hell, they might not even end well if it is Maddox. So I suggest you run. And don't worry, I have a map of the ship so I can tell you where to go."

My arms and legs tingled, and my heart quadrupled in time as adrenaline spiked through my system. "I don't want to run. I told you—"

"I played along, let you see Maddox again. And now that you have, now that you know his feelings for you aren't what you want, we can leave and never think about him again."

"I'm not staying here for Maddox," I protested.

Or am I? I'd gained so much ground in the short amount of time since I'd figuratively come back to life. But my journey was nowhere close to being complete. Even though Maddox had been the trigger for my awakening, it was possible that he'd become a hindrance.

Grinding my teeth together, I came to a decision. I wouldn't lead my life for Maddox, my family, my people ... no one but myself. Not anymore. I had goals and dreams—the need for closure and peace. I wouldn't accomplish any of it if I kept worrying about Maddox.

The time to be selfish is now. Bending low, I waved my hand in a flourish. "Lead the way, Ressi."

Giggling with glee, her clothes pixilized before changing to an all-leather Steampunk pants ensemble, complete with top hat. Again, it looked suspiciously similar to one of Jane's outfits. I stifled the urge to roll my eyes. "What?" she huffed. "It's my escape outfit. Too bad you don't have one."

I glanced down at my nondescript clothes. I wore black leather pants, a black tank top, and black leather boots. "None of that matters. Now, let's go."

Ressi's expression twisted with disdain, and I could tell she wanted to disagree with me, but she somehow resisted an outburst. Her whiskers trembled with the effort. "This way." She flew out in front of me, the fur on her face parting as if blown by wind.

Keeping pace behind my A.I., we raced through a small corridor before coming to a slender metal ladder. "I wasn't brought down this way."

"This is the back way. Less chance of running into anyone," Ressi responded before floating upwards.

I hesitated only a moment before scurrying up after her. I remembered hearing Maddox go up a ladder the last time he left my cell room. "Are you scanning for lifeforms?"

"Of course," Ressi snapped. "This isn't my first rodeo. I — Eeep!"

"What? What is it?"

Ressi appeared right by my ear. "Abort! Abort! Get the hell back in Dodge ASAP!"

"Ha! I knew you couldn't be trusted!" Cora's blonde head poked into view.

Without thought, I reached up and grabbed her by the front of her shirt. "And Maddox told you to stay the hell away from me," I snarled. Yanking hard, I pulled her through the space in the floor at the top of the ladder. She scrambled to latch onto me or the ladder, but her positioning was awkward, and my momentum carried her head first towards the floor. I hooked my boots under a rung as I flipped over, my back slamming into the corner of the ladder, shoving all the air from my lungs.

I hung there gasping for breath, upside down, my ears ringing, and my vision spinning. *Come on. You can do this.*

Get a move on. Gritting my teeth, I used my abs to raise myself up so I could grab onto one of the rungs. Once I was righted, I glanced over my shoulder. On the floor, crumpled in a heap was Cora. A small pool of blood was forming around her head.

"Shit," I muttered. "Is she dead?"

"Afraid so," Ressi said, her lavender gaze fixated on Cora's body.

My stomach roiled, bile racing up my throat. "I didn't – I shouldn't have— Shit." I pounded my fist against the ladder, the pain centering me. "What's done is done. No time for lingering. Especially now." Tearing my gaze away from Cora's greying face, I completed my climb. As I sprinted after Ressi, her small form a blur, another wave of dizziness assaulted me, causing me to stagger.

"Come on, hurry up! We don't have much time! According to the ship's central computer, there should be several escape pods—"

"Nina?" Skidding to a stop, I swung my gaze over my shoulder, meeting Maddox's golden orbs. Confusion skittered across his visage. "What the hell are you doing?"

My heart fluttered in my chest. *What will he do when he finds out I killed Cora?* "I think it's pretty obvious what I'm doing."

Lifting his nose, he sniffed the air in the direction we'd come from. "Is that blood?" His lip curled back, revealing small fangs. "Cora's blood?"

Shit. "How do you— What ... You can smell her blood?" What was he now? What had they done to him?

Maddox closed the distance between us in two long strides. "What the fuck did you do?"

I lifted my chin in defiance. "I didn't mean to hurt her. She came at me and I simply reacted."

He grabbed my wrists. "But you didn't just hurt her, did you?"

I could tell by the rage burning in his eyes that it wasn't a question. He somehow already knew the outcome of my and Cora's altercation. "No. She's dead."

His jaw muscles rippled, a low growl vibrating in his chest. "I can't let you leave."

Sweat trickled down my spine, pooling in the hollow of my lower back. "You think you can stop me?"

"No doubt about it."

"Hmm," I grunted. Killing Cora had changed everything. No matter what information I claimed to have, or how much Maddox championed me, if I stayed on his ship, it was only a matter of time before I'd be dead.

Desperate times call for desperate measures.

Lunging into Maddox, I wrenched my arms up, breaking free from his grasp. But instead of making a break for it like he expected, I brought my knee up to his crotch, at the same time bringing my fist to his temple. Dropping to his knees, his expression went blank, and he crumpled to the ground.

I laughed. "I can't believe that worked."

"Me either," Ressi said, hovering over Maddox's unconscious body. "Now let's go."

"Not without him." A plan was formulating. One that

was every bit as crazy as I seemed to be in that moment. "We're going to need him."

"Need him? Need him for what? Did you hit your head on the ladder? Is that what this is about?"

"Shut up and find something to help me lift him. He's coming with us." I tapped my chin. "Oh, and something to bind him would be helpful, too. You know, for when he wakes up."

"Nina, no. I can't let you—"

"Just do it!"

Ressi flitted off, grumbling about me having lost my mind. I grinned. She was probably right. But the good news was, sometimes insanity and genius were two sides of the same coin.

Chapter 5

Sweat leaked from every pore on my body. My muscles spasmed with exertion, the tendons in my neck straining. "Who would have thought he'd be so damn heavy?" I gritted out between clenched teeth.

Ressi snorted. "I don't know, like anyone who has eyes. He's over two hundred pounds of solid muscle."

I glanced back at the door to the escape pod I was attempting to lift an unconscious Maddox into. We'd managed to transport him this far by way of a cart with wheels. The last few feet were turning out to be the difficult ones. I refused to give up though. He was my hostage and he was coming with us. End of story.

"Just leave him. We don't have much time. I'm surprised we haven't been discovered yet. But luck won't stay on our side for long, especially not with a dead body lying around."

"Aaaaah!" Losing my footing, I fell onto the floor, Maddox slumping on top of me. I stared at the ceiling, panting. "I'm not giving up. I just need to get him into the pod."

Ressi sighed. "You really do have a death wish, don't you? Or are you just that obsessed? I mean, you're literally abducting him. You knocked him out and you're—"

"I get it. I know what I did. I don't need a recap." Hefting myself up, I continued to inch my way towards the pod, my arms wrapped firmly around Maddox's middle, his head resting against my chest. Skittering backwards I slipped again. "Motherfucker!" I slammed my fist against the floor. Letting loose another string of obscenities, I pulled us up again. "This is happening. Did you hear me Universe? This is happening, so you can take your laws of gravity and shove them up your ass!"

"Now she's arguing with gravity. Great," Ressi muttered, but obviously, she meant for me to hear her.

Sucking in raspy breaths, I continued my battle until finally, I managed to get Maddox into the pod. It was definitely an act of God. No less than a miracle. I paused to stare at Maddox's form slumped over in the pilot seat of the escape pod. *Or maybe not. Shiiit. How am I supposed to get him over to the other seat?* My arm muscles trembled in protest at just the thought. But I couldn't exactly fly the pod with him in the pilot's seat. *Or can I?*

Scurrying all the way into the pod, I closed the door behind me. Wriggling into Maddox's lap, I yanked the harness around both of us, strapping us in for the flight. It was a tight fit, but it would have to do.

"You can't fly like that!" Ressi shouted, bouncing around the interior of the pod. "It's not—"

"I don't see a problem. I mean, we fit, and I can reach all of the controls." To demonstrate, I fired up the thrusters, preparing for takeoff.

"And when he wakes up, even cuffed, he'll be able to easily overpower you and turn us right around. Do you want this to be an effort in futility?"

"We'll be fine." I punched in the launch code, which was standard, and we jettisoned into the air, the pod shaking violently.

Maddox groaned, mumbling something indiscernible.

"He's waking up!" Ressi yelled, her ears flattening with panic.

Wrenching to the side, I slammed my fist into his temple. His head lolled on his shoulders, and his mouth fell open, drool dripping from the corner. "Sorry," I mumbled. It wasn't like I wanted to hurt Maddox, but I couldn't deal with him at the moment.

"You can't keep doing that unless you want to give him brain damage," Ressi chastised.

"He'll be fine."

"Oh, right, because he probably already has brain damage so you won't notice a difference. I get it. Carry on."

Banking to the left, I narrowly missed the top of a tree. I wanted to stay low on Zeffrin until I got to the other side of the planet, where I'd make a run for space. Zooming right off the planet would have been a rookie mistake, garnering unwanted attention from New Earth soldiers who were on high alert. Even now the chances of us getting caught were most likely. Which was why I'd brought Maddox along. With him as a hostage, the chances of us getting shot down were slim. Although his presence didn't absolutely guarantee our safe passage.

I'll probably end up getting us both killed. Ressi's right. I have lost my mind.

Oh, well, too late.

Maddox groaned again, the muscles in his chest quivering when he attempted to lift his restrained arms. His nostrils flared as he sucked in a pained breath. "Nina," he mumbled. "Wh-what happened?"

"Shhh, everything is going to be fine. You just need to sleep. I'll explain everything when you wake up."

"No. I can't sleep. Something's wrong ... something—" His eyes flew open, darting around to take in the situation, and he snarled, "What the hell did you do?"

Panicking, I slammed my fist into the side of his temple, watching in horror as he slumped over, unconscious once again. "Shit. I didn't mean to do that."

Ressi perched on the control panel, shaking her head. "I was joking before about the brain damage, now, I'm not so sure."

Grimacing, I shot furtive glances at Maddox as I navigated across Zeffrin. "Maybe this was a bad idea." I nibbled on my bottom lip, double-checking the pod's radar to make sure no one was following us. Coast was clear … so far.

"*Maybe* it was a bad idea? I think it definitely—"

"Back in the band," I hissed, waving my wrist.

Ressi's nose scrunched. "You do realize that I don't actually go 'back in the band', right? You do realize that I'm still—"

"I don't care. I just don't want to look at your stupid, judgey face right now. So … Back. In. The. Band. Now."

Ressi popped out of sight, but not before sticking her tongue out at me.

Heaving a sigh of relief, I shifted forward, my ass rubbing along Maddox's muscular thighs. I shivered, and my stomach flip-flopped as my temperature shot up a few degrees. It was shameful how my body reacted to the contact. For God's sake, the man was unconscious and my blood was heating from sitting on his legs, not even from being in his lap. *Pathetic.* Although I was only human, and humans had physical needs, and not just sexual in nature. I snorted. *Sexual in nature.* Hell, I couldn't even remember the last time I'd been touched in a mildly affectionate manner, let alone anything sexual.

When did I start thinking of myself as fully human, or at least labeling myself as one? I considered the question as I swooped up and around a steep hill. I guess it was when I'd turned my dearly departed husband over to Jane. That was when I'd truly begun thinking of myself as something other than a Denard. I'd wanted separation from the vile creatures, even if it was simply in my mind. But I knew the truth ... call me human or Denard, I carried the same monstrous DNA within my system.

Shaking my head to clear my thoughts, I glanced back at Maddox again. He was still out cold, a steady stream of drool trickling down his chin. My lips curled up as I stifled a laugh.

"There's something wrong with this picture," Ressi's disembodied voice stated with annoyance. "I feel like you should be the one with drool on your chin. How about you stop staring and figure out where we're going? I noticed you haven't punched in any coordinates for a destination yet."

"Quiet. I'm thinking."

"Yes, I know, about Maddox. And by the way, your heart rate has accelerated I'm pretty sure it's about him being naked. It would be nice if—"

Fumbling for the switch hidden on the underside of my wristband beneath a secondary panel, I shut down my annoying sidekick with a flick of my finger. Sometimes she could be a bit much. She'd be spitting mad when I rebooted her, but it was a small price to pay for some temporary solitude.

"Now, where the hell do we go?" I muttered to myself.

We didn't have a ton of options, actually, none that I could think of at the moment. *Shit. There has to be somewhere.* There was a reason I'd been hanging around on The Pittsburgh despite my general unwelcome status. Dar, the massive Gartian, had made it crystal clear that I needed to watch my back when it came to him. Not that I blamed him, after all, the Denards had nearly wiped out his entire species. Things like that usually generated animosity.

Pinching the bridge of my nose, I kept the pod steady with my other hand. I needed to come to a decision soon or we'd end up circling back around to where we started. *Just pick somewhere, damnit ... anywhere. Death is guaranteed here, but at least you have a shot out there.*

Coming to a decision, I forced my trembling fingers to enter the code. *This is a bad idea. So bad.* But as soon as I finished, the tiny pod was shooting into space, and it was too late to change my mind.

Chapter 6

Maddox groaned and shifted. "Nina, I really hope when I open my eyes that you knocking me out and abducting me was all just a bad dream."

Nibbling my bottom lip, I glanced out the small window as space blurred by. I opened and shut my mouth a few times, nothing but a squeak coming out. The truth was, I had no idea how to talk to Maddox anymore. I wanted to be able to tell him everything, all the while encircled in his comforting arms, but that wasn't going to happen.

Maddox sighed, his lids slitting open. "Why? Why would you do this? I told you all you had to do was lie and I'd have your back. Now there's no way—"

"I didn't mean to kill her. Cora. I didn't mean to kill Cora. She was lurking around my cell again, and when I tried to make a break for it, there she was. I reacted on instinct, pulling her off the ladder. Her head broke the fall." Sliding out from under the harness, I flopped into the other seat. I didn't need to worry about flying the pod any longer since the autopilot was engaged. *And continuing to sit on Maddox isn't helping anyone, least of all my libido.*

Maddox and I stared at each other, the moment stretching into an eternity. Finally, he cleared his throat. "I believe you. It's just— Fuck. Cora was a part of my … team, and her death was needless. All of this is in fact."

"I couldn't sit in a New Earth cell waiting for the other shoe to drop. I have too much to do and not enough time to accomplish any of it."

"Nina, my people need me. You have to send me back."

I shook my head. "No. I can't. Besides, not to insult you or anything, but you're just one man. And Special Ops or New Wave, whatever you are now, at that. You going missing for a bit won't turn the tide of this war one way or another."

"You have no idea what you're talking about. If I'm not—"

"He's right. You have absolutely no idea what you're doing anymore, Nina."

Ressi's furry Steampunk-clad body hovered between Maddox and me, her back to him, and her whiskers twitching with annoyance.

I flipped over my wristband, glaring at it. "How'd you do it? Huh? How'd you reboot yourself?"

Ressi shrugged, her ears flicking back. "Maybe I was never off to begin with. Maybe I had a feeling that you would do something stupid like try to make life-altering decisions without me."

"You don't have feelings! Not real ones! You're a goddamned A.I.!"

She drew up her tiny paws in front of her chest. "That hurts, Nina. A knife right here in my heart."

I rolled my eyes. "You don't have a physical body. How many times do we have to go over this? You—"

"Um … I am having a nightmare, aren't I?" Maddox interjected. "Complete with insane miniature cat-people. I would really like to wake up now."

Ressi wheeled on him, her chest heaving. "It's not my fault I look like this! I was designed to be endearing to a five-year-old!"

Maddox leaned to the side, his gaze meeting mine. "Or am I the one who's lost their mind? You hit me too hard? Are you even really here? Am I?"

Slumping in my seat, I tipped my head back. "Everybody calm down. Maddox, you're not insane. Yes, you really are here, as am I, and Ressi, who happens to be my A.I."

"Then you need to take me back!" Maddox roared. "Whatever you're planning I can't be a part of it! I have responsibilities! I'm not the same stupid kid you knew all those years ago!"

I dug my fingers into the armrest, my knuckles aching. "No. I already told you that I can't take you back."

"Nina, please … just please." He may have verbally pleaded, but his golden eyes burned as if they could force me to bow down to him from their mere force of will. "You don't understand. They need me."

I stared out the tiny window, not wanting to look at his face. *He's the one who doesn't understand.* A few weeks ago—or was it months, not that it mattered—I would have been happy to die. I would have done anything to end the meager existence I'd been forced to have with my husband Ambassador Aralias. But things had changed, and now I wanted to live ... truly live, not simply exist anymore.

"I need to fix things," I whispered. "I need to fix everything."

"You told me you didn't know anything. Someone without any connections or information can't fix a war, Nina." Maddox's voice had taken on a cajoling tone, one that had the opposite effect on me.

"I don't have information or connections ... yet. But there has to be something I can do." I slammed my fists against my thighs repeatedly. The pain was welcome, helping to focus me. "I want to wipe them out. All of them."

"You want to wipe out the Denards? Your people?"

"They're not my people anymore!" Blood pounded against my eardrums, my vision wavering. I sucked in several deep breaths before turning to Maddox again. "They're monsters and they deserve to die."

"Okay," Maddox drawled as if he was addressing a child. "So where are we going then?" He glanced at the control panel and then back to me.

"To Anzax."

His left eye twitched. "To Anzax."

"Yes. The Anzaxians aren't part of the UGFS alliance, not aligned with us or the Denards. They—"

"There's a reason they aren't part of the UGFS and they still exist. They're—"

"Lethal. Dangerous. I know." I shifted forward in my seat. "But if we could convince them to help us—"

"It's not going to happen. We'll be dead before we can even land on their planet." He twisted to the side, his shoulder muscles bulging. "Uncuff me, Nina. Now. I'm done playing this game."

Ressi's eyes widened, and she disappeared abruptly. My blood went from a simmer to a full-out boil. "Game? You think I'm under the impression that this is all a game? You think I don't fully understand what's going on out there?" I waved my hand towards the window. "You think I can't comprehend the enormity of what's happening in our Universe?"

A growl rattled inside Maddox's chest. "No, I don't think—"

Standing, I poked Maddox in the sternum with my index finger. "I wasn't done." I bared my teeth. "You might not like it, any of it, but you're my prisoner and you don't get a say in what happens from this moment on. You will do everything I say, no questions asked, because that's what prisoners do."

His jaw muscles rippled as he ground his teeth together audibly. "Is that what you did when you were his prisoner? Whatever he wanted, no questions asked?"

Maddox's words filtered into my brain slowly, but when they penetrated fully … My fist shot up to slam into his temple. Shock emptied all other emotions, and then his face went slack and he slumped back into his seat.

"Shit," I mumbled. "I can't believe I did that again."

Ressi's laugh filled the air. "He's going to be even more pissed when he wakes up. But damn, your aim is on point with that. Out cold with one hit every time. I'm kind of impressed."

I stared at Maddox's now passive face. Sweat glistened around the edges of his short hair, his angular features softer at rest, and flushed from his recent bout of anger. My fingers itched to trace the contours of his high cheekbones. *I could stare at him all day.* I sighed. *Why can't we go back to the way it was before? I don't want him to be a stranger to me.*

"So Anzax, huh?" Ressi perched on Maddox's shoulder, arms and legs crossed. "It pains me to say it, but I agree with the douche on this." She poked him in the cheek with her elbow. "You're going to get us all killed if we go there."

"You'll be fine. You know, because you aren't actually alive."

"I really wish you would stop saying that when you're mad at me. You know A.I. is aware. Maybe we aren't alive in the traditional sense, but it's close enough."

I grunted in response, not wanting to have an existential discussion with her about what life really is. We'd had it before and I lost every time. She still hadn't managed to sway my opinion though. Ressi was merely better at debating than I ever would be, she did have a computer for a brain after all. "I know Anzax is a risk. A big one. But I don't have any better ideas, do you?"

"Anzaxians aren't whispered about at supply space stations like the tales of the Gartians. The Gartians were steeped in mystery, which was why they were feared, but they were still predictable. Stay out of their territory and they'd leave you alone. The Anzaxians," she shuddered, all of her fur standing on end, "they've been seen. Usually committing brutal acts of murder or heinous crimes. Not to mention they aren't even the tiniest bit humanoid in appearance. Oh, and they don't have the UGFS mandatory translator implants either. How are we even supposed to communicate with them if we get that far?"

Translator implants. Shit. I'd forgotten about that part. Gnawing on my thumbnail, I considered. "Well, I can understand them, so that's half of it. Can't you download a translator program and be my go-between?"

Ressi slapped her palm against her forehead. "Now why didn't I think of that?" She rose into the air as she rolled her eyes. "I know!" She snapped her fingers. "Because I can't download their language when it's unknown. No such program exists."

"Oh."

"We need a new plan. End of story."

"I don't have one, and we can't just float through space indefinitely so I made a choice."

"So change your mind!"

Flipping over my wristband, I eyed the switch that was

supposed to shut Ressi down. I flicked it off and on a few times, Ressi remaining fully visible in her 3D hologram. "How'd you disable it?"

She shrugged, studying her nails.

"Fine, don't tell me, but you better go ahead and re-enable it."

"No."

I quirked an eyebrow. "No? You're telling me—"

Staccato beeps erupted from the control panel just as the pod lurched to the left, sending me sprawling across Maddox. I scrambled to slip back under the harness. "What's happening?" The navigation system was going crazy, dials and meters spinning out of control.

"Someone has us!" Ressi bounced around the pod, scanning. "But it's not a standard tractor beam, it's some kind of magnet."

"Magnets? Who uses those anymore?"

"Lunins," Maddox mumbled, his eyes still shut. "Lunins still use them."

"I have no data in my records on any species called Lunins," Ressi said. "What the hell are they? Are they dangerous?" Her ears flattened. "Oh my God, are we about to die?"

Maddox groaned, his thighs tensing underneath my ass. "Me. They probably sense me like I sense them."

I tilted my head to try and see something, but only stars and empty space filled the window. "How do they sense you?"

Snarling, Maddox's muscles strained. "No. Stop. Not

here." His eyes flew open, the gold in them glowing like twin flashlights.

My hands flitted around his face, not knowing what to do or what was going on. "What's happening? What's wrong?"

His lips curled back to reveal elongated eyeteeth that resembled fangs. Chest heaving, his muscles doubled in size, his shoulders straining to break free of his bindings. "Get away from me now," he growled, his voice unrecognizable. Hair sprouted all over his face and visible skin, the audible sound of bones popping and rearranging as his features and body changed shape.

Sliding out from under the harness, I backed away, plastering myself against the other side of the pod. "What's happening?" I raised my hand, covering my open mouth where a scream lodged.

The pod spun, throwing me against the window, before dropping me abruptly to the ground. My head thumped against something sharp, black spots filling my vision. I managed to grab the edge of the seat, pulling myself towards it.

The pod veered to the right, and I slid across the floor, slamming into the wall. An inhuman howl met my ears just as everything went dark.

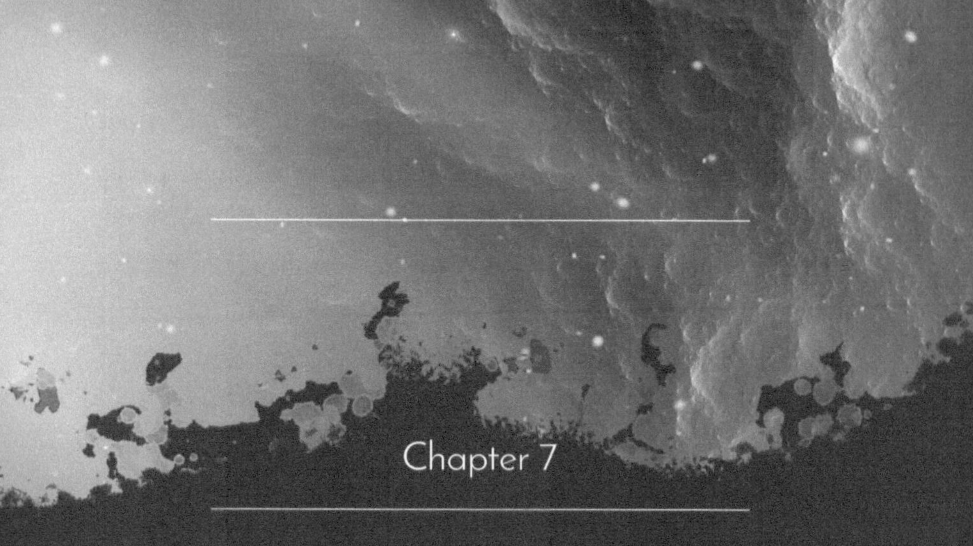

Chapter 7

"Get rid of her. She's not of our concern." A masculine voice penetrated my consciousness.

A low growl followed by a ferocious snarl pounded against my skull. I groaned.

"Nina. Nina," Ressi whispered into my ear. "You need to wake up. This is serious. Maddox transformed into some kind of wolf mutant, and I think the Lunins want to throw you out into space, best case scenario."

Warmth suffused my side, a solid mass pressing into me. I groaned again, running my fingers along my scalp. Wincing, I found two small bumps, but thankfully, neither seemed to be bleeding.

"What happened?" I muttered.

Fuzzy images of Maddox turning into … something—something inhuman, flashed across my brain. *No. No, that can't be right.* My eyelids popped open, adrenaline shoving me into a sitting position. My heart stuttered and then took off at a gallop, slamming against my ribcage. I was just outside our pod, sprawled on the rusty metal floor, with a large, chocolate-colored, wolfman-creature hovering next to me. His face remained humanoid, albeit covered in fur, golden eyes glowing. Nearly doubled in size, Maddox had sprouted wolf ears, and his hands had grown long black claws. His clothes hung from him in tatters, bits of fur sticking out in all directions.

He's a monster.

Surrounding us in a half circle were several male humanoids, all of their eyes glowing with the same golden hue. They were decked out in dark brown leather from head to toe. The one in the center, directly in front of us, took a step forward, his gaze accessing. He was taller than the others, hair as dark as midnight, long and shaggy, hanging around his pale face. "There seems to be some kind of force field around them."

That's right. I'd almost forgotten about Maddox's talent to throw up a protective force field. It used to be his only ability, which was why he'd been a Class 2. His new man-wolf development would explain the change to Class 4.

Another one of the Lunins spoke. He was short and stocky with golden hair pulled back in a low ponytail, his complexion tawny. "He's not like us. He's human, or was. Maybe spliced with DNA from another species besides ours. Or he could have been bitten, however unlikely."

The tall one replied, "He's enough like us that we

sensed him. An injured tribe member. It's our duty to at least attempt to help him."

Someone snorted.

Waving my hands in the air, I cleared my throat. "Can you understand me?" Who knew if the Lunins had translator implants or could understand my language? I internally crossed my fingers that there wouldn't be a communication barrier.

The tall Lunin's lip curled. "Of course we can understand you. We're not primitives."

It took all of my willpower to not bring up the whole magnet thing. Their equipment was so outdated, that it would definitely be considered primitive. "Okay, good. I think there's been some kind of mistake. We—"

Maddox backed up, bumping into my side, a low chuffing noise escaping him. I blinked several times, not sure what to do.

"I am Xorik." The tall Lunin bowed slightly. "You need to tell your mate to calm down. We mean you no harm. We only wish to help him … and you."

Ressi buzzed around my head. "Then what was the talk about getting rid of her?" she demanded.

Xorik smiled, his gaze remaining cold. "Nance didn't mean it. He didn't realize the situation."

Tilting my head, I scanned the Lunins. They definitely weren't friendly, but they were better than Anzaxians. Of course, almost any species would be better than the Anzaxians. "And what situation would that be?"

"You are clearly important to him. Either you already

are his mate," he nodded at Maddox, "or his intended. It's not something we take lightly."

The left side of my face twitched. *Mate? As in friend?* Even with the implants sometimes things were still lost in translation. "I don't understand."

Xorik glanced at Nance, a silent directive passing between them. "Come, have him drop his shield and we will take this conversation to somewhere more comfortable. Somewhere with food."

As if on cue, my stomach growled. *Oh, come on. I just ate a little while ago.* My body always betrayed me in one way or another. "I have no control over what Maddox does. You're going to have to convince him that you mean us no harm."

Xorik studied Maddox, whose breathing had evened out a bit. "Is this his first shift?"

"I'm not sure. But I don't think so. He seemed to know what was happening to him even if I didn't." He'd demanded that I get away from him. Why? Was he afraid I'd be scared, or was he worried that I actually had a reason to be? At the moment, despite his horrific appearance, I wasn't afraid of him. In fact, his presence had the effect it always did … I felt safe with him, even when I wasn't sure what I meant to him anymore.

Xorik dropped down into a crouch, his gaze meeting Maddox's. "Shift back now to your human form." His voice was calm, the tone even, but it carried a command with it interlaced with power.

Maddox dropped to the ground, his eyes rolling into

the back of his head. His mouth opened in a silent scream as he arched up sharply. Fangs shortened back to blunt human teeth. Fur retracted, and bones popped as his muscles shrank. Within a few minutes, Maddox—my Maddox—lay half-naked on the floor in front of me.

"Neens … I'm sorry." He reached out to touch me, his arm flopping to the ground before he could make contact. His eyes fluttered shut.

Gasping, I scooted on my hands and knees, closing the scant distance between us. "Maddox. Are you okay?" I ran my fingers along his neck and chest. His skin was like ice, but covered in a fine sheen of sweat. "Maddox?"

"He'll be fine," Xorik stated. "He just needs some rest. A forced change is taxing on the body."

"Forced change?" Tears stung the corners of my eyes, and I blinked furiously to keep them at bay. "I don't understand any of this." *What's been done to you, Maddox? Why did you let them do this? Why?*

"Come." I was lifted to my feet by strong hands. "You will eat and talk to me while he rests. I will help you to understand what's happening with your mate. And you will share what you know with me."

He keeps calling me Maddox's mate. I needed to get to the bottom of that, amongst other things. "How do I know I can trust you? Any of you?"

"You don't. But you don't have a choice."

Ressi had disappeared. I had no doubt she was already attempting to hack into the Lunin central computer for information. There wasn't much I could do in my current situation. Xorik was right. I would have to trust them for the time being because I didn't have any other alternatives.

"All right." I lifted my chin. "But only because I'm hungry."

Xorik's lips curled up, his features softening slightly. "A female after my own heart. Follow me." He stalked out of the room, obviously expecting me to obey him.

Grimacing, I paused, shuffling after him a moment later. *Please don't let this end in all of our deaths.*

Chapter 8

The Lunin ship, name unknown, was … antiquated. Surfaces covered in rust and dirt, I was surprised the old bucket of bolts was keeping us afloat and alive in space.

After my limited tour, aka my trek from the pod to my current location, I found myself sitting at a small, grimy table near what could be considered a kitchen. Xorik sat across from me, his hands steepled in front of his mouth. His gaze danced from the plate set in front of me, heaped with untouched food, to my face, and then back again.

Swallowing bile, with shaking hands I pushed the plate to the center of the table. "I guess I'm not hungry after all." At least for raw meat from an unknown animal. *Is it Lunin fare or are they simply fucking with me?*

Xorik tilted his head, his eyebrows lifting. "You're lying. Do you not find the food to your liking?"

I sputtered on a laugh. "Um, I hope I don't insult your

culture by saying this, but no. I don't generally chow down on raw meat. I prefer my food cooked, and not still bleeding."

He grunted, shifting in his chair. "Tommy, get in here, boy."

A tall, lanky Lunin with pale hair and skin hurried into the room, his head bowed. "Yes, Xorik?"

He motioned to my plate. "You need to cook this meat for our guest. She doesn't—"

"You want me to cook it?" Tommy gaped at him. "But why? It's some of our best—"

"Don't question me, boy. Just do it."

Standing, I waved my arms back and forth. "Hey. No. Stop. That's okay. Don't waste good meat on me. I don't want it even if it is cooked." Both men turned towards me, and my face heated. "Don't you have pasta of some kind?"

"Pasta?" Tommy's voice went up a few octaves. "You want pasta? I don't even know what that is."

I wasn't surprised. Pasta originated on Earth, and it was difficult to come by since the destruction of the planet. "Don't you have anything that didn't used to be alive?"

Xorik snorted. "All food used to be alive. Even vegetation once lived."

Slumping back into my seat I stared at Xorik, narrowing my eyes. "Now I know you're fucking with me. What's your problem? Messing with my meal is not the way to get on my good side. It's not like I asked for food, you offered."

Xorik smirked. "All right. Tommy, bring her something that will suit her delicate pallet. Something a herbivore would enjoy."

Tommy scurried out of sight, chuckling under his breath.

I scowled. "I'm not hungry anymore. You can take your faux hospitality and shove it up your ass." Slapping my hand over my mouth, my eyes widened. I hadn't meant to say the second part out loud. It was generally not a brilliant idea to insult the Lunin who could just as easily kill you as help you. "I-I'm sorry. I didn't mean that."

"Yes, you did." He lifted his head, nostrils flaring. "And yet I don't detect any fear, simply," he sniffed the air," worry. Interesting."

Yeah, I'm worried you're going to kill me. I may be a little off my rocker, but I'm not a complete idiot. "Look, let's be honest. I don't want to be here, and you clearly don't want me here. What do I have to do to be on my way? With Maddox of course."

"Your mate isn't going anywhere. He is a Lunin now, and here is where he'll stay."

My heart quadrupled in time, and my stomach twisted. Swallowing several times around the lump in my throat, I found my voice. "No. You can't have him. I won't let you." *I'll fight to the death for him if I have to.*

Xorik drummed his fingers along the table. "Very interesting indeed. Now you smell of fear. So you don't fear for yourself, but for your dear Maddox?"

"He's not meant to be here. He's New Earth Special

Ops—or First Wave—I'm not even sure anymore," I muttered, "but his people need him." Guilt pushed at me as I used Maddox's words against Xorik. If it wasn't for me then Maddox wouldn't be in this precarious situation to begin with. I'd screwed up royally when I decided to take him.

"Lie," Xorik stated calmly. "But which part?" Tilting his head back and forth, he studied me.

Slapping my hands against the table, I grimaced. *How the hell can he tell I'm lying from my scent? Is it some kind of wolf thing?* I wasn't sure what they were exactly, but I had already begun forming theories about the Lunins. *I need information from him. But shit, this conversation is not going to be easy with a living lie detector.* "Okay fine. I don't actually believe his people need him. At least not right away. He is only one man. And it isn't like he's commander of the First Wave or something. But he doesn't belong here, and he can't stay."

"Truth."

"No shit," I snapped. "Why would you want to take someone in who you don't even know? Who are you Lunins? I've never heard mention of you until we were locked in your tractor beam."

Xorik nodded. "We like to fly under the radar. I'm surprised Maddox knew of us. That does answer a few questions. He was not bitten but made." Frowning, a low growl trickled from his throat. "But it doesn't matter. He's here now and here he will stay."

"I don't know if you've gotten the news or not, but

there's a war going on out there. There's no way Maddox will just give up on his people."

"We are his people now."

We're getting nowhere fast with this. "But who the hell are you? I thought you said you were going to explain to me about Maddox."

Xorik shifted, his golden eyes blazing with mirth. "I also said that you would share what you know with me."

Why is he toying with me like this? What's the point? "You're not even asking me anything. Not really. You're just fucking with me."

"I would say that I'm sorry, but I'm not. It's been a long time since we've had any sort of visitors." He leaned back in his chair, propping his booted feet on the edge of the table. "And it is in the Lunin nature to … fuck with people, as you put it. We think of it as having a bit of fun. Obviously, you do not."

"Obviously," I grumbled.

The entire situation was surreal. One moment I was hurtling through space with Maddox in tow, and the next I was on a ship filled with a species I'd never heard of before. And a strange one at that. They appeared humanoid on the surface, but there was something distinctively savage and animalistic simmering a few layers down.

"Tell me," Xorik said. "What do you know of Maddox's condition? I suspect he wasn't bitten, and that the scientists on New Earth have been tinkering with human genetics again, but it's hard to tell for sure without more information."

I didn't trust Xorik, but it seemed pointless to hide what little I did know about Maddox. "He told me that something had been done to him to make him less human. He said he'd volunteered for it to help his people. But until he shifted into that ... until he changed into whatever he was, I had no idea what he was referring to. I'm not sure what you mean by being bitten, but it seems to me that you're right about the New Earth scientists."

"You smell human," Xorik interjected. "And yet you keep referring to New Earth and its people as if you are not from there."

He didn't ask, but the question was there unspoken. I gulped, my temperature rising a few degrees. "I was born ... elsewhere. So I don't think of them as my people. In fact, I don't have any people. Not anymore." There was no way I was going to admit to my origins. The truth would probably get me killed. Even if the Lunins flew under the radar, not caring to be involved in politics, there weren't many fans of the Denards. They simply excelled at making enemies.

His eyes gleamed. "So you are one hundred percent human? You haven't been spliced in any way like the citizens of New Earth?"

Nibbling on my bottom lip, I nodded. "Yes, I'm human. One hundred percent."

"And you are not mated to Maddox, nor has he declared his intentions to claim you?"

Claim me? And what is up with this mate thing? Why does he keep bringing the term up? "How many different ways do I have to say it? I'm human. And no, I'm no one's mate."

A smile slowly crept across Xorik's face, his white teeth catching the light. "Exactly what I wanted to hear."

Warning bells erupted inside of me. I sensed danger, my adrenaline spiking. *But why? Nothing seems amiss.* "Explain." My hands fisted, wishing for a weapon, any kind of weapon. The duffle bag I'd taken off The Pittsburgh with me had been full of them. I suddenly felt like unsuspecting prey caught in Xorik's predatory sights, completely helpless and alone.

He sprung to his feet, prowling around the table towards me. Scrambling back, my chair clattered to the floor. "Calm down, little human. Don't make this any harder than it needs to be."

I dropped into a fighting stance. *Damn, I swear I'd sell my soul for a laser gun right about now.* "Stay where you are!"

Xorik chuckled, his eyes sparking with delight. "I'm glad I didn't listen to Nance about you. He wanted to put you back in your pod and throw you out into space." His eyeteeth lengthened into fangs. "But I had a feeling about you."

Well, shit. None of that sounds good. "Stay back!"

Ignoring me, he tapped his tongue against one of his fangs. "I wanted to do it right there, but I had to be sure. I shouldn't have doubted my instincts."

My back hit the wall, and I glanced around wildly. "I said to stay the hell away from me!" But my words were just that … words. I had no weapons, no special training or skills. Sure, I was good in a fight, but I knew I wouldn't be able to hold my own against Xorik with nothing but my fists.

In a blur of motion, I found myself caged in by Xorik's massive frame. Golden eyes blazed as they bore into mine. "Don't be afraid. It'll be over quickly. At least this part will be."

"Don't be afraid, wife. It'll all be over quickly." Amir's phantom voice ricocheted through my mind. Screaming with rage, I butted my head against Xorik's chin, at the same time bringing my knee up to connect with his crotch. Staggering back, he clutched himself, snarling.

I spun, dashing out of the door. I'd only managed to get a few feet before I was slammed face first into the floor. Dazed, the coppery tang of blood running down my throat, I thrashed in an attempt to dislodge Xorik from my back.

His large hand palmed my head, wrenching it to the side. Pain shot through my neck, and I screamed, reaching behind me to claw at Xorik's face. *Is he—is he biting me?* "Get off me! Get the hell off of me!"

"Stay still. You're only going to make it worse," he growled against my flesh.

Amir's voice filled my head. *"I don't know why you fight me. I always win."*

"No!" I screeched. "Noooo!" Bucking, Xorik fell off of me, and I scrambled to my feet. Black pushed into my vision around the edges, and I staggered. "No, no, no, no, no." Amir's face danced in front of me. I punched at it, falling forward. "No. You're dead. Leave me the fuck alone."

Hands grabbed me from behind. "Calm down. You're only going to hurt yourself."

I couldn't breathe, and my heart was about to explode from my chest. "Don't touch me! Don't ever touch me again!"

Fresh pain tore at my neck. What little air I had left in my lungs was sucked out.

Everything went dark.

Chapter 9

"Nina, do what you're told. You know what happens when you disobey me."

Hanging my head, I turned from my husband. I wanted to fight him, but I'd learned the hard way that it would only make things worse for me. I was a coward, wishing to avoid pain even if it meant subjecting someone else to it. I had no one to turn to, no one who would aid me if I tried to run. I was trapped. The best I could hope for was a quick death.

"Yes," I croaked, pursing my lips.

"Now."

I risked a glance at the woman chained to Amir's bed. She was humanoid, small, and blonde, and if I was honest, she resembled me in more than one way. Scars littered her face and body, my husband's fun leaving her close to death. And yet he wasn't done. Guilt washed over me. I can save her. It's not too late. *I knew what the cost would be, though—I'd end up on the receiving end of the torture she would have received.*

Dropping to my knees, I tugged at my husband's hands. "Please, Amir, why do you do this? It's a sickness. You can find help. I—" His knuckles connected with my cheekbone, sending me sprawling. I groaned into the plush carpet, tensing for what was sure to come next. Why? Why do I bother? I knew this would happen. Maybe I want to die? At least it would be an escape. No more pain. No more guilt. Just the bliss of oblivion.

The edge of his boot connected with my hip. Pain lanced up my side, and I curled into a ball. "You think I'm sick? You? The woman who fucked a hu-mutt?" His boot found my back next, agony shooting up my spine. "My whore of a wife thinks to pass judgment on me?" Gripping my hair, he wrenched my head back. "This is your fault." Spittle hit my face. "All of it. I can't kill you because of your father, so I torture women who look like you. I wish it was you on that bed." His eyes overflowed with hatred. "And when her last breath rattles from her chest, I'll wish it was you." Slamming my head into the floor, he let me go. "I've never hated anyone or anything as much as I hate you, my dear little wife."

"Then do it!" I screamed. "Kill me! Just get it over with! Kill me now!"

Amir chuckled. "Oh, but that's another reason why I won't. Because it's what you want. It would be too easy. I would much rather keep you alive ... and suffering."

Clawing my way back to consciousness, my eyes fluttered open to take in an old, rusty ceiling. Groaning, I swiped at the sweat that was pebbled along my forehead and upper lip.

"Nina," Ressi whispered, "thank God you're awake. We're in trouble."

My head throbbed in time with my pulse, like someone had done a little jig on my skull, and a dull roar had taken up residence in my ears. I attempted to sit up but found myself unable to muster the energy.

I licked my dry lips. "Ressi, talk to me. What's going on?"

Flitting into view to fill my vision, she peered down at me with ears pinned tightly against her head, and her eyes wide with worry. "That—that monster threw you into this cell with a gaping wound in your neck."

Gasping, I brought my hand up to my neck. The skin was unmarred. Confusion rushed through me. At Ressi's prompting, I remembered the attack, and yes, the bite. "Who healed me then?"

"It closed quickly, but something's not right. My readings on you are off, like something's changing in you. We need to get—"

"Well, well, well, what do we have here?"

Ressi squeaked and pixilated into nothing. Fresh adrenaline gave me the energy I'd been lacking before, and I staggered to my feet. "Let me the hell out of here." I'd apparently traded my cell on Maddox's ship for one on Xorik's. Only my new quarters were much smaller, and definitely not state-of-the-art.

Xorik tilted his head to study me. "You should lie down. Things will get worse before they get better." He actually had the nerve to appear concerned.

Gripping a set of bars, rust abraded against my palms. "Why am I in here? Where's Maddox?"

"Your friend is fine, but you don't need to worry about him anymore."

"Oh, so now he's my friend and not my mate? You better start talking, wolf boy."

Xorik threw his head back and laughed. "Wolf boy. I like that. And I like how you're not afraid of me. Not intimidated in the least. Even after what transpired between us."

My chest tightened as the memory of him attacking me wove together with memories of my husband. "I'll kill you for what you did to me, just like I did him."

"You can try. I hear the mating process is extremely fulfilling when the female doesn't simply fall over onto her back." His eyes glimmered with heat, trailing along every curve of my body. "Tell me, where did you get those scars?"

My nostrils flared, and I ground my teeth together, gripping the bars even tighter. "None of you damn business where I got my scars. I—"

"No need to be ashamed," he interjected. "They were one of the things that first drew me to you. You are like no female I've ever come across before. You are a warrior."

"You know nothing about me. And if you like them, I'll be sure to have them removed as soon as possible."

A corner of his lip curled up. "Remove them if you wish. But they will forever remain in my mind as a testament to your strength."

I didn't want to share where I'd gotten the scars, but if it helped put an end to Xorik's attention, I'd do what I had to. "I'm not strong. I didn't get these scars in any way that you can possibly be imagining." My hands dropped to my sides as I stepped away from the bars. "My husband, or ex-husband, he's dead now, he gave them to me. He tortured me for years in fact, and I let him."

A choked sob wrenched from my chest as an image from my recent nightmare played out in my mind's eye. *"I've never hated anyone or anything as much as I hate you, my dear little wife."* I inhaled the scent of my blood and sweat, unable to tell if it was the past haunting me or from my recent dilemma.

Tugging on my hair, I met Xorik's gaze. "I just let him." *Don't show him your emotions. Just keep to the facts.* Steeling myself, I sucked in a few ragged breaths. "So whatever your preconceived ideas of me are, let them go, and let me go, too, while you're at it."

"You killed him … your ex-husband."

Not a question, but a statement. "Not exactly."

He waved his hand at me in dismissal. "No need to fuss over all of this. I already know all there is to know about Ambassador Aralias, and his ex-wife, Nina Aralias. You may not see it as I do, but you're a survivor, and therefore a warrior. It may have taken some time, but in the end, you triumphed. Warriors come in all shapes and sizes, metaphorically speaking in this instance. I have no falsely preconceived ideas about who you are, although maybe you do."

Choking on my own spit, I stumbled back, hitting my shoulder into the wall. "How do you know his name or mine? And the rest, how did you know the rest? Did Maddox tell you?" And why the hell was he asking me questions he already knew the answers to? Was it more of his mind games? He couldn't seem to get enough of them.

He shook his head, an arrogant smirk teasing his full lips. "No. Maddox remains in a healing slumber."

"Then how?" Did Lunins have mind reading abilities? They could sniff out the truth, or at least Xorik could, but mind reading was on an entirely different level. *Shit. Things keep going from bad to worse.*

"I delved into your mind when I gave you my bite. An Alpha like me can do many, many things that other Lunins cannot." His gaze slid over me again with blatant carnal suggestion.

Shit. Not only did he read my mind, but he went into my past. Just the thought of him kicking around in my head caused my chest to tighten, and my muscles to lock up completely. I'd been violated before, in a multitude of ways, but this was something I'd never experienced until now. My mind had always been mine and mine alone. The one place I could escape to without fail.

No. Stop. I forced myself to take a deep, shuddering breath, the oxygen burning my lungs. There was no time for my neurosis. I had to find out what was going on so I could come up with an escape plan. "You need to stop being so damn cryptic and tell me what exactly Lunins are, and what the hell you want with me."

Crossing his arms, Xorik leaned against the wall, his gaze locking with mine. "We adopted the name of Lunin because of how Earth's moon once affected our ancestors. Since it no longer exists, it has no sway over us, and we've changed because of it. We're stronger, more in control than we ever were on Earth."

He lifted his dark brows as if waiting for me to connect the dots. When I didn't he continued. "There was Earth lore, mostly rumors of what we were, but even back then no one had it right. We were once called—"

And then it all clicked. "Werewolves," I finished for him. *Fuck. Me.* Not only were they from Earth, which definitely made them a target and therefore an enemy of the Denards, but they were supernatural creatures. How did I never hear of them before? Did the Denards think they'd wiped them out like the phoenixes? Because if they did, then obviously they'd failed on both accounts.

He smirked. "Yes. So you've heard of us?"

"Well, I've heard the rumors at least." My trembling hand found the spot on my neck where he'd bitten me. *Please let that part be a part of the lore and nothing more.*

Taking in the placement of my hand, Xorik tilted his head. "I'm afraid that part is true. A bite from one of us, at least an Alpha such as myself, can turn a full-blooded human into a Lunin." He grinned. "Welcome to my pack, Nina."

"No." I shook my head, my eyes widening. "Huh-uh. I don't want to be a Lunin." Rushing forward, I slammed my palms against the bars. "I don't want to be a Lunin, and I don't want to be in your pack. I don't want any of it." I punctuated my declaration with several more hits against the bars. The rusty metal thudded under my assault, pieces of rust burrowing into my flesh. *This is all a nightmare. I'm still in the pod. I hit my head. That's all. Soon I'll wake up. Wake up, damnit. Wake up.*

"It's too late to go back now. I've bitten you, and soon you will begin to change."

My chest heaved from exertion as I continued to bloody my palms against the bars. *Nightmare. It has to be a nightmare. Please don't let this be happening. I won't let it happen. Nightmare ... nightmare ... nightmare. Wake the fuck up, Nina!* But deep down in my gut, I knew the truth. "No! I won't let anyone take my life choices from me ever again! I'll rip you to pieces with my bare hands before I let that happen!" A red haze dropped down in front of my vision, guttural snarls ripping from my throat. "I make my own choices! Not you! Not anyone else ever again!"

"Nance!" Xorik called.

A moment later, the blond Lunin from before entered the room, a pissed-off expression on his face. "You don't have to yell in and out of my head. I heard you the first time."

Xorik scowled. "Then you should move faster." He motioned to me. "Administer the serum. It's time."

"Let me out of here!" I snarled, the sound of my voice startling me. It was inhuman and guttural ... a stranger's. "Now! Let me out now!" Sudden pain ripped through my abdomen, causing me to double over.

"Do it now," Xorik commanded, "before it gets worse."

"I hope you're not planning on babying her all the time because that'll get old real quick."

Babying me? Was he fucking kidding? Uncurling from my hunched over position, I met Nance's gaze, baring my teeth. "I'm going to kill you, too."

He grinned. "Okay, she's kind of growing on me. She's definitely going to keep you busy."

"No one is going to be busy because you'll all be—"

"Yeah, yeah. We'll all be dead. Time for you to take a little nap." Nance lifted a gun and pointed it at me. "Sweet dreams, killer." He pulled the trigger.

A whoosh of air and a sting in my forearm drew my gaze to a metallic cylinder embedded partly in my skin. "What the—"

Dizziness slammed into me, and my knees buckled. Xorik and Nance's voices warbled, the words becoming foreign to me. My eyelids slid closed, the weight of them too much for me to bear.

I floated away on a cloud of darkness.

Chapter 10

Pain. Deformed hands. Claws. My hands?
Pain. Bones breaking. Am I dying?
Pain. Blood. My blood?
Pain. Screams. My screams?
Pain. Agony. Who am I?

MUMBLING SOMETHING INCOHERENT, I opened my eyes slowly, even that small movement difficult. My entire body ached, like I'd run fifty miles and gotten into a fight with a Gartian when I was done.

My tongue was heavy, filling up my mouth. "Thirsty," I moaned. My head was lifted, and a tin pushed up against my lips. I lapped greedily at the cool liquid, the taste of it sweet.

My thoughts were muddled, my brain foggy. The only

image I could conjure was of Maddox, his beautiful face and bemused expression dancing across my mind. "Where is he? Where is Maddox? I need him." A deep-seated yearning tore at my chest, ripping me open and leaving me raw.

"You don't need him. I'm here," a familiar masculine voice responded, although I couldn't quite place it.

Fury built within me. "Don't tell me what I do or do not need. It's my call because it's my life." *I always have a choice. Always.* With that thought came clarity. Something I hadn't had in a very long time, if ever.

I'd believed that my mother had forced me to end my relationship with Maddox. That I didn't have a choice. I'd been convinced that my husband had stolen my will, trapping me with him. I thought he'd taken away my power to choose. I'd believed myself a victim of so many, but the truth was … I'd only ever been a victim of myself. I'd had choices and options. I simply hadn't been brave enough to accept the possible consequences of my actions. There is always a choice. *Even if someone puts a laser gun to my head, I can choose death over something I don't want to do.*

No one took my life choices from me. I gave them away. I let myself be swept away by things I believed were more powerful than me. *No more.* Maddox showing up on The Pittsburgh had awakened something dormant within me. That something had been burned, killed, and buried in a billion different ways. He made me feel again, which I refused to lose. But in the end, I was responsible for how my life ended up, not Maddox … not anyone. I was done blaming others for things that were of my own doing.

Slapping at hands curled under my head, I drew on energy from deep down to sit up, my vision swimming. "I asked you a question and I expect an answer. Where is Maddox?"

Xorik's lupine features came into focus, his head tilted as he studied me. He was perched on the end of the cot in my cell, still so close I could feel his body heat. "Nance, is Maddox awake yet?"

Inhaling, I realized my sense of smell was sharper. Each individual note was pulled through my nose and settled on my tongue so I could taste it all as well. Images of what happened in my cell when I was unconscious shifted through my mind. I'd changed. Morphed into a wolf creature of my own before slipping back into my human skin. Xorik and Nance had tended to me, making the transition as easy as possible, administering a serum every so often to aid me in sleeping so I wouldn't be in constant pain. They'd also changed my translator implants to a special kind that could withstand the shift between forms. With everything else going on within my body, it had been the perfect time. Relief washed over me to know that I wouldn't be left without a way to communicate easily.

Blinking, I realized I'd been so focused on my scent memories that Nance had disappeared, and Xorik was standing. Exhaustion pulled at me. The time for fighting would be later, for now, I just wanted answers. "Will it be like that every time? The pain and confusion?"

"No. Eventually the shift to your other form will be easy and you will be able to do it at will and in an instant."

I quirked an eyebrow. "What about Maddox? It didn't seem easy for him."

"I doubt he's shifted more than a few times, if that. We found blockers on him that he'd been administering to halt the change completely. If the scientists of New Earth spliced some of their soldiers with Lunin DNA, they probably didn't want them wolfing out in a battle so they figured out a way to control it."

"Why didn't the blockers work for Maddox before? On the pod?"

"He has to receive a dose in regular intervals. Obviously, he missed a dose. Although he may have burned through it faster than normal because of the stress he was under."

I tugged at my hair, my scalp aching. So his unscheduled and unwanted shift into a wolf-creature was my fault for abducting him without listening to a damn word he said. He'd tried to warn me that he had to go back, but I ignored him completely. Guilt swept through me. *No. Let it go. What's done is done. It's what you do from this moment forward that matters. Your choice. Always.*

"Is Maddox different from you? Am I?"

Xorik scratched his face, shifting back and forth from foot to foot. He clearly was over the Q and A portion of our conversation. "Some Lunins are born, like me. Both of my parents were Lunin, which is why I'm stronger. But then others, such as Nance and you, are changed from a bite. Although only a born can create a bitten. All of us, Maddox included, have partial human DNA. But Maddox is something else entirely. Something new. He was spliced before the Lunin DNA was introduced to his system. I'm not sure what it will mean for him in the long run."

"But how can a bite alter DNA? None of it makes sense." Maybe back in primitive times, before gene splicing and space travel, things like that were believed because no one had the ability to study any of it. But with all the modern technology we now have, it all seemed a bit … silly.

His lips curled up at the corners. "Magic rarely makes sense."

"Magic, really?" I scoffed. Although I did remember Zula saying that magic was still a satisfactory way to explain away things that even science couldn't explain yet.

"I have to say, you're taking all of this well. I'm a bit surprised after you threatened to kill me repeatedly and in great detail." His eyes glimmered, the challenge in them unmistakable.

"With war on the horizon, I don't have time for an emotional breakdown." At least another one. I'd had plenty over the last few months, and I was sure after everything finally settled, I was due for another huge one.

"This war, it has no bearing on you anymore."

My pulse thrummed a staccato beat against my eardrums, my skin tightening, and my gums itching. I opened my mouth to reply, but my lower lip caught on ... fangs? My eyes widened as I traced my tongue over that new development. "How do I make them go away?" I demanded, although I wasn't sure my words were more than a connection of incongruent consonants and vowels.

"Calm down. Strong emotions trigger the change in the beginning. You'll learn to control it."

Claws dug into my palms as I curled my hands into fists. *I don't have time for this shit.* "The war has everything to do with me. If you've been kicking around in my head like you claim then you should understand."

Xorik rolled his eyes. "I understand that you're young, and you have no concept of what's truly important."

Young? How old was he exactly? Were Lunins a long-lived species? Did that make my life span significantly longer now that I was one of them? "And what do you think is truly important, oh old and wise one?"

"Survival."

I narrowed my eyes. The more information I got, the more I needed. "Why did you turn me? What do you want from me?"

Pushing off the wall, he prowled towards me, his eyes glinting. "I thought I already made myself clear. I want you for my mate."

Sweat trickled down my spine, my muscles bunching with tension. "And if I don't want you?"

He swept a long finger under my chin, tipping it up farther. "And why wouldn't you? I'm Alpha."

Shuddering, I backed up, and his hand fell to his side, a

frown marring his features. I wasn't used to being touched, at least not in a non-threatening manner. I hated how a part of me craved more, despite who was doling out the attention. "Like that makes a difference to me. You can't just bite me and think my entire belief system is going to change. I was human a few hours ago."

"Days. It's been three days."

Days? Well, shit. No wonder I feel like someone landed a hovercraft on me. "Hours or days, it doesn't matter. My opinion on things hasn't changed just because my DNA has. This war is important to me. I'm not going to simply forget about it and play house on this bucket of bolts with you."

He snorted. "Bucket of bolts? I see. You think we don't have resources. I can assure you that isn't the case. We have an old ship and equipment because it helps us blend in. Shiny things draw attention."

"Don't care. I'm not going to be your mate. End of story. So don't even think about laying your paws on me again."

He opened his mouth to respond, his brows furrowed with anger, but he didn't get the chance. The ship rumbled and lurched, the lights blinking off and then on again.

Jane's voice crackled over the intercom, barely discernable. "Lis-en up. I'm Cap-n Ja Wexis an you betr han over Ni and dox."

"What the fuck?" Xorik growled.

Ressi appeared behind his head. She stuck her tongue out at him and made a face. I snickered. "In case you couldn't understand that, I'll translate. Captain Jane Wexis of The Pittsburgh is here and she demands that you turn Maddox and me over to her."

Nance raced into the room, skidding to a stop on the other side of the cell. "Xorik, there's a crazy phoenix woman in our control center threatening to roast all of us alive if we don't give them Nina and Maddox." He pointed at Ressi. "That thing is back!"

"Thing? I'm not a thing!" she exclaimed. "I'm an A.I., and it's not my fault I look like a cat person. I was designed to be cute to a five-year-old."

"I should have had it dismantled," Xorik growled. "I knew it was a mistake not to. Her A.I. is the one who contacted this Jane, I have no doubt." Nance held the door open as he stalked through it. "I'll deal with the phoenix. You stay here with her."

Ressi bobbled around the cell, her whiskers and tail twitching. "Did you hear him, Nina? He wanted to dismantle me. Me. Just like that, I could have been poof, gone."

Picking up the metal cuff that housed Ressi's electronic components off the floor near my cot, I slid it back on my wrist and secured it. I was surprised Xorik hadn't destroyed it. Actually, I was shocked that he'd even known what it was to decide not to. Maybe he wasn't as dumb as I thought when it came to technology. It was possible that what he'd said was true and they simply preferred out-of-date things to fly under the radar.

Keeping his gaze fixated on the door, Nance addressed

me. "I knew you were going to be trouble from the first moment I laid eyes on you."

I grinned. "Thanks, I'll take that as a compliment."

I perched on the edge of the cot, tugging at my new clothes. I was now encased in dark brown leather like the rest of the Lunins. Apparently, Xorik had taken it upon himself to dress me when I was out cold. I was thankful after my old stuff was shredded from the change that he hadn't left me naked. With what he had in mind, I wouldn't have been surprised. It seemed as if his cockiness had worked to my advantage though. He'd clothed me because he obviously didn't think it would be difficult to get me naked and underneath him whenever he felt like it. I snorted. He was in for one rude awakening.

I swiveled, staring at the entrance to my prison, anticipation zinging through my system.

Now I wait for Jane to make her grand entrance. She never disappoints.

Chapter 11

Flames spewed around the corner from the hallway, ashes raining down on Nance's head. Eyes wide, he danced an odd little jig, arms and legs moving back and forth rapidly, as if he was afraid he was going to spontaneously combust.

Doubling over, my stomach cramped as a full-body laugh consumed me. Just as I'd thought, Jane was making her entrance in a grand manner. She was nothing if not dramatic.

Nance was cowering in the corner, pressed up against my cell by the time she strode into the room in all of her Steampunk glory, complete with a top hat perched on her head.

"Oh, come on. I thought you all were big, bad, wolfy men. Or is it a dog thing? Afraid of fire?" Flames danced along her arms, and Nance whimpered, covering his head.

Ready to be free, I bounced up on the balls of my feet. "Maddox ... did you find Maddox?"

"Ash should have him on The Pittsburgh by now. So, shhh, don't spoil my fun." She loomed over Nance, who curled into himself tighter.

Grimacing, I bit my tongue to keep quiet. Jane and I had a tentative truce. If I pissed her off I had no doubt she'd leave me right where I was to rot. "What happened to Xorik?"

"Xorik? Was he the supposed Alpha who thought he could take me down?"

"Probably."

Nance whimpered. "Please, I'll let you take her. Just— I need to attend to my Alpha. I can feel him calling me through our bond."

Pressing my fingers into my scalp, I scowled. I sure as shit hoped Xorik wouldn't be able to communicate with me through any kind of Lunin bond. After all, his bite was the one that changed me. I stalked forward, grabbing Nance by his hair through the bars. "Will he be able to get into my head?" I wrenched him to his feet, slamming his shoulders against the rusty metal. "Tell me if he'll be able to get into my head."

Fangs sprouted from Nance's mouth, and fur sprang from the pores on his face. I slammed him several more times, eliciting a series of terrified yowls from him, his eyes flitting back and forth between Jane and me. "Don't you dare change on me when I'm asking you a question. Will he be able to get into my head?"

"Hey. Stop playing with my toy," Jane demanded. "It's been a while since I've gotten to go on a hunt and this is the next best thing."

"Back off," I snarled, fangs protruding over my bottom lip. *Shit.*

"Ladies." Ash's smooth voice drew our attention. He stood by the door, his muscular arms crossed over his chest. "Can't I leave you unsupervised for a minute, Jane?"

Her flames went out instantly, and she waved her arms around in frustration. "Stop doing that, Ash! You have no right to steal my fire!"

He smirked. "Then don't abuse it."

"Just wait until I figure out how to do it back to you. Just you wait." She slammed past him, stomping her way down the corridor.

I dropped Nance, who scurried from the room on all fours.

Ash eyed me. "What trouble did you get yourself into now?"

Scratching my head, I glanced away. "Oh, nothing much. I just got bitten by an Alpha Lunin who has decided he wants me for a mate."

Ash's blond eyebrows shot up to his hairline. "Interesting."

We stared at each other. Ash had never hidden the fact that he disliked me because I was a Denard, and because I'd been married to Ambassador Aralias specifically. But he'd gone along, or been forced, by Jane to accept me aboard The Pittsburgh. I knew her choice to hoist me off on Maddox had been a welcome one by him.

He cleared his throat. "I guess I better let you out of there so we can get a move on. We have other more important things to worry about." He shot a flame ball at the lock on my cell door, the rusty thing swinging open on contact.

Shuffling along, I followed Ash as he led the way to The Pittsburgh. "Maddox is okay, right?" I wasn't sure if Jane would have said anything to me if he wasn't. She was well aware of how I felt about him. I couldn't shake the nagging feeling that something was wrong with him.

"He was unconscious, but other than that he seemed fine. Tamzea and Eron were already tending to him when I left."

I nodded. Maddox was in good hands with Tamzea and Eron. Mazatimz healers could fix things that no other species could. "But it didn't seem like anything had been done to him?"

Ash held the airlock door open for me. "I'm not sure what you mean. He was unconscious. But I didn't see any bruises or blood. Nothing to indicate anything had been done to him beyond whatever knocked him out."

"Xorik said he was in a healing sleep. But it's been days." I gnawed on my thumbnail, my fangs having retracted somewhere along the line. "I—"

Maddox's scent slapped me in the face. I'd noticed immediately the way my sense of smell had been heightened exponentially since Xorik's little love bite, although most things kind of blended into the background unless I was concentrating. But this … this was … unlike anything I'd experienced before.

His scent conjured images of him. Hands sliding along my bare flesh, heated kisses and hot breath warming my skin. I shivered with delight, needing to get to him. I was driven, focused. Nothing else mattered more than surrounding myself with him and reveling in his unique perfume. He was safety and security, comfort and warmth … he was home.

My legs carried me of their own accord, no conscious command needed. As I tracked him, I considered … Describing someone's—anyone's— personal aroma was not something I'd thought about much in my lifetime. Scent was usually either a positive or negative thing. Maddox had always smelled good, spicy and warm in some indefinable manner, but now I picked up on notes of cinnamon and dark chocolate. A combination that normally would seem unpleasant, but in his case, it blended to form the most perfect scent imaginable.

Bursting into the medical wing, I rushed past Tamzea, who protested my abrupt arrival, and threw myself at Maddox. He was sprawled across a cot in the far corner of the infirmary, his eyes closed, and his breathing even. Pressing my nose along his neck, I inhaled, sighing with delight.

"Nina." Tamzea tugged at me. "You don't want to accidentally injure him. We still—"

"Leave me alone." I slapped at her hands blindly,

burrowing in closer to Maddox. He was safe, and I merely wanted to hold him in my arms to make sure he stayed that way. Nothing else mattered in that moment.

"Nina, please." Tamzea tugged gently at me again. "He needs his rest."

"Leave her alone, Tamzy," Eron said. "She's not going to hurt him. You worry too much."

"But—"

"If it was me on that cot, would anything drag you away?"

Tamzea released me, the soft pads of her footsteps gliding across the floor as her answer.

"Maddox," I whispered. "I'm sorry. I'm so sorry …" Choking back on a sob, I brushed my nose back and forth against his skin. "I've been doing everything wrong. And I'm sorry I dragged you into it."

"Nina?" Pushing myself up onto my elbows, I peered down at Maddox, his eyes slitting open, and his brown eyes sparking with gold. "What happened?"

Cupping his stubble roughened cheeks, I plastered what I hoped was a smile on my face. "Don't worry about any of that right now. You have to rest."

His brow furrowed. "No. The Denards … the war …" His eyes fluttered shut. "You smell different," he murmured. "Like my Nina … but better."

My Nina? Disbelief mingled with hope within me. "Some things have changed while you were sleeping. I'm like you now."

He made an odd chuffing sound, one side of his mouth twisting up. "Mmm … not like me … better."

I blinked. *Better? What does he mean by that?* "Maddox, I know you probably won't remember this and it's a hell of a time to confess it, but … but—" I swallowed, gathering my courage. "I love you. I'm not sure I ever stopped. Even, or maybe, especially when I was with him. I thought—No. That's not right." I took his large hand within mine, squeezing it. "I wanted to love Amir. It would have been easy if I did. And in the beginning, he was so charming, I thought … well, I thought that I could forget you. I thought I loved him, but I didn't. I couldn't." Falling onto his chest, I slid my arms under him. "I wonder if you could ever care about me again? Maybe even love me?"

His heart thrummed rapidly beneath my ear. "Nina," he whispered. "There's never been anyone else in my heart but you. No. No one but you." He choked back on a laugh. "You should have seen Cora's face when I said your name when I was inside her. It's why she hated you so much."

I sucked in a sharp breath, my heart turning to ice. *What did he just say? When he was inside of her? As in they'd had sex?* My right eye twitched, and I disentangled myself from him. Staring down at Maddox … I suddenly wanted to smash his face in, irrational jealously choking me. *Stop. She's dead, and you killed her.*

And I'd kill her again if I could.

"Nina." Maddox reached for me, his hand falling to his side as I backed up. He didn't seem to notice in his half-awake, partly delirious state. "Come back. I want to hold you."

My nostrils flared as I attempted to hamper my growing rage. Claws sprouted from my fingertips despite my best efforts. "No. I have to go now. You need your rest."

"Nina. My Nina." His head lolled to the side as his breathing evened out.

A low growl rattled its way up through my chest. He'd fucked Cora? When was the last time they'd been together? Had it been when I'd been locked up on his ship?

An overwhelming and foreign urge to sniff him for her scent washed over me. *When was the last time he showered?* Bending over his crotch, I inhaled. *Nothing.* Pressing closer, I sniffed again. *Nope. Just his scent. Nothing else.* But I had to be sure.

"Wh-what are you doing?" Jane exclaimed, her tone loud and sharp.

Grimacing, I sucked my bottom lip between my teeth and slowly turned around. There in the doorway stood Jane and Zula, both of their faces scrunched up with confusion ... yeah, and barely contained laughter.

Jane clutched at her stomach, her body quivering. "Were you just smelling Maddox's man bits?"

"No. I was just ..." But what could I say? There was no feasible explanation for what they'd caught me doing. I'd been caught red-handed—or maybe I should say, red nosed, all up in Maddox's crotch. It would have been one thing if they'd interrupted something sexual, but clearly, with him unconscious I couldn't even claim an odd fetish. My crazy was showing and everyone in that room knew it.

"Ash said you were bitten by a Lunin, and so—" Zula doubled over, her blue-tinged skin taking on a lavender shade. "It makes sense if you were scenting him. Wolf shifters or werewolves, whatever you want to call them, often act instinctually like their animal counterparts. Scent is very important to them." She glanced at Jane, sputtering, "Sh-she was probably j-just scenting him." A high-pitched squeak escaped her mouth before she could shut it, her skin darkening to indigo as she erupted into laughter a moment later.

"Riiight. Scenting him. Makes perfect sense." Jane threw her arm around her. "I've never seen you laugh like this before. You're making up the scent thing, aren't you?"

Zula sputtered and giggled, attempting to scowl, but failed horribly. "No. Not making it up. I've just never actually seen someone sniff … she was … she was sniffing his … man bits."

They both collapsed to the floor in a heap, laughing. I narrowed my eyes, unsure if they were actually that amused or they were putting on a show to harass me.

"I was doing no such thing." Notching my chin up, I stepped around them, leaving all three infuriating creatures behind me.

I swear, if having a family means putting up with people like Jane and Zula, I'm not sure I'll ever want one.

Chapter 12

A smile tugged at my lips, pulling down into a scowl, and then swinging back up into a smile again. My emotions were just as unstable as my current facial expressions, waffling between humor and anger. The scene in the infirmary had been … amusing, and yet the whole thing pissed me off.

Flopping onto my back in bed, I stared at the ceiling. I'd locked myself away in one of the spare living quarters; the one that had been mine before Jane had unceremoniously booted me off the ship. I didn't want to face any of them … Jane, Ash, Zula, Kade, Tamzea, Eron, Masha, and especially not Dar. *Wow. The Pittsburgh's crew is really filling out.* There'd been a time when it'd been just Jane, Zula, Tamzea, and Masha, an all-female crew with Jane heading it up as their bounty-hunting captain. Their lives had gone sideways the moment Jane had decided to take the exclusive contract on Ash offered by my now deceased husband.

That contract had changed my life, too. It'd been the catalyst for … everything. *Where would I be now if she'd turned it down?* I shuddered to even consider it. With one seemingly small choice, Jane had changed the path of all of our lives, and countless others. It was a ripple effect that had grown into an asteroid storm.

I flopped over onto my stomach, fighting the urge to visit Maddox again. I hadn't been back since the crotch-sniffing incident. No doubt Jane and Zula had shared the story with Tamzea by now. I had no desire to see the knowing gleam in her eyes if I found my way back there. All three of them, Jane, Zula, and Tamzea, had become like sisters to each other. Masha was one of them, too, although she was like the odd Guaviva sibling, always remaining on the outskirts of things, a part of it, and yet decidedly separate. It was completely her choice though. Guavivas were odd creatures, interested in machines more than personal interaction, which worked out perfectly for Dar since he was a cyborg.

I sighed, attempting to manage my wayward thoughts. However, they circled back around, and I sighed again. I wasn't sure if they even realized it, but as someone on the outside looking in, it was as clear as day on Mercury. They'd grown and learned from each other, changed, forming a family of sorts. Some would argue the change was because they were all paired off, Jane with Ash, Zula with Kade, Tamzea with Eron, and Masha with Dar, but that wasn't the case at all. They'd found the strength to go after happiness because of the changes they'd helped cultivate in each other.

And I was jealous.

Rolling onto my side, I growled. My mind was everywhere and nowhere all at once in an attempt to not think about Maddox ... and Cora. The irrational fury that had burned through my system remained, simmering just below the surface. *She's dead. Let it go.* Yet I couldn't help but wonder if they'd had a relationship. I wasn't sure why it mattered, but it did. Somehow, it would soothe me to know that Maddox had merely been fucking her, as opposed to being legitimately involved with her. Sharing his body with Cora was one thing—we all had urges and needs, and we hadn't been together—but opening his heart ... *No. He could never have feelings for someone like her.*

"Nina, please stop with the angst. You're going to fry my circuits." Ressi curled up beside me, a thin, furry arm flung over her face. "I kind of wish I wouldn't have disabled my shutdown switch. I could use a break right about now."

I flicked her nose, my fingers passing through her. "You think I like feeling this way? You think I enjoy obsessing about Maddox in bed with *her*?" My words brought up an unbidden image of them naked and entangled, sweaty bodies writhing in ecstasy. "Stop," I grumbled, pressing my palms into my eyes. "I need to get it out of my head."

"Hmmm ... so now that you're back on The Pittsburgh,

thanks to me, and we don't have to worry about insane Lunins or murderous Anzaxians, what's your plan? I assume you still want to," she raised her hand to make air quotes, "stop this war, and get your revenge against your people who you no longer claim as your people."

"They aren't my people anymore in my mind, or in actuality. I've become a Lunin. The Denards would shun me now that I'm like this, even if I wanted to go back, which clearly I don't."

Ressi's tail swished back and forth. "Huh. Yeah, I guess you're right. I hadn't thought about that. Guess it's a good thing you already decided to abandon your roots."

Is that what I'd done? Abandoned my roots? That phrase made it seem like a negative thing. Like I'd turned my back on who I was. *But if who you are is a monster, then it's definitely a good thing.* Or was I merely turning the hate I'd been raised to have against the Denards, unable to truly let it go? *Is hate in any form a good thing?*

Well shit, I'm teetering dangerously close to some sort of existential crisis, I can feel it.

Squinting at Ressi, I noticed she'd coded herself a new Steampunk outfit. "So, have you been doing anything productive? Or are you following Jane around for fashion inspiration?"

"Hey! I—"

Her voice faded, a sharp jab to my skull stealing my attention. A flash of Xorik in my head preceded his arrogant voice. "Nance told me you'd been asking if I could get into your mind. Does this answer your question?"

"Fuck," I growled, rubbing my temples. My living quarters were still visible, Ressi chattering away completely unaware that my mind was under siege, but my attention was forcibly focused on Xorik. "What the hell do you want?"

"Mmm … I think you already know the answer to that."

"But why me? I'm sure there are plenty of willing Lunin females who would welcome your attention."

"Not as many as you think. Very few female babies are born naturally, and pure-blooded humans don't exist anymore. Or at least that's what I thought until I met you."

Shit, shit, shit. There was nothing like a shortage of females to send any species into a psychotic tizzy. Xorik didn't necessarily want *me* per se, just what I was. No wonder he was so quick to jump into changing me … literally.

A flash. A muddled image. Spliced human women who exhibited no powers, all Class 1, abducted from New Earth, and changed in the same manner as I had been. But it hadn't been Xorik, no. It'd been … "Your father!" I exclaimed. "He stole women from New Earth and changed them against their will?" But it wasn't a question. I was already aware of the sordid details. They came to me in another flash, faster, as if the information was simply uploaded straight into my brain. In that instant, I also knew how New Earth scientists had come by the genetic material needed to splice Maddox's DNA.

"Yes," Xorik confirmed. "My father never came back from New Earth. It's been over a decade. I assumed him dead."

"And he may very well be. New Earth scientists don't need live specimens to do what they do." I paused, shifting through the plethora of information to find what I wanted. "But you didn't follow in his footsteps … and your species has been dying out because of it."

"Our species now."

Snorting, I ignored him. "I was like a friggin' gift showing up the way I did. I might as well have had a bow wrapped around me."

He chuckled. "And I find myself attracted to you. Win-win as far as I'm concerned."

Win-win for who? Certainly not me. Ignoring him again, I pressed forward in my search for information. "But Nance had wanted to get rid of me. He—"

"His mother was an abducted New Earth woman. They were both taken when he was just a child. He's loyal to me and our kind, but he hated my father. He was afraid of what you would bring out in me. He was afraid to discover I'm just like my father."

"Hmm … well, okay. Sounds to me like you should leave me alone then. Unless you actually do want to be like your father, then you need to not force yourself on unreceptive women. Or woman … basically I don't want you, so go away."

My mind filled with laughter. "I would never force myself on you. I—"

"Then what was with the bite and being kept in a friggin' cell?"

"The confinement was for your protection during the change. As for the bite … you would have asked for it eventually."

The man was seriously delusional. "How exactly do you figure that?"

"Once I seduced you, you would never have wanted to leave my side. I simply did things out of order because of how eager I was. I yearn for a mate … and an heir."

Scratch that, not simply delusional. Add in arrogance to create a toxic combination that equaled stalker potential. *I'm going to need to be painfully blunt with him.* "Nope. Not happening. There will be no heir provided by me. I have a war to deal with. And like I already stated … I don't want you."

"Knock, knock!" Jane's voice wafted through my door. "Get your ass to the eating lounge for a meeting." She kicked the door, her steel-toed boot thunking menacingly. "And stop disabling the intercom in your quarters. Masha is going to have a mental breakdown. Plus, I'm the friggin' captain, not an errand girl! I'm not going to fetch you whenever I need you!"

"I'll be right there!" I briefly turned my focus inward again, confirming the connection broken between Xorik and me. Ressi had disappeared as well, probably pissed off because she'd finally noticed I hadn't been listening to her.

Either that or she was up to no good. Either scenario wouldn't end well for me.

Sighing, I sat up and yanked on my boots. I didn't need the added complication of an obsessed Lunin with unidentified supernatural abilities. Trepidation swirled in my gut. I wasn't privy to most of the details of how Jane and Ash had gotten together, but Zula still made snarky comments about how Ash had simply decided to mate her … and boom, they were mated. Could Xorik do that to me?

No. Jane simply resisted the bond, but she'd wanted Ash just as much as he wanted her from the beginning. *The only Lunin I have any desire for is Maddox.* But what if he ultimately doesn't want me?

No. Stop. Now is not the time to think about any of this. Lurching to my feet, I ambled out of my quarters, heading to the meeting, which promised to be its own brand of torture.

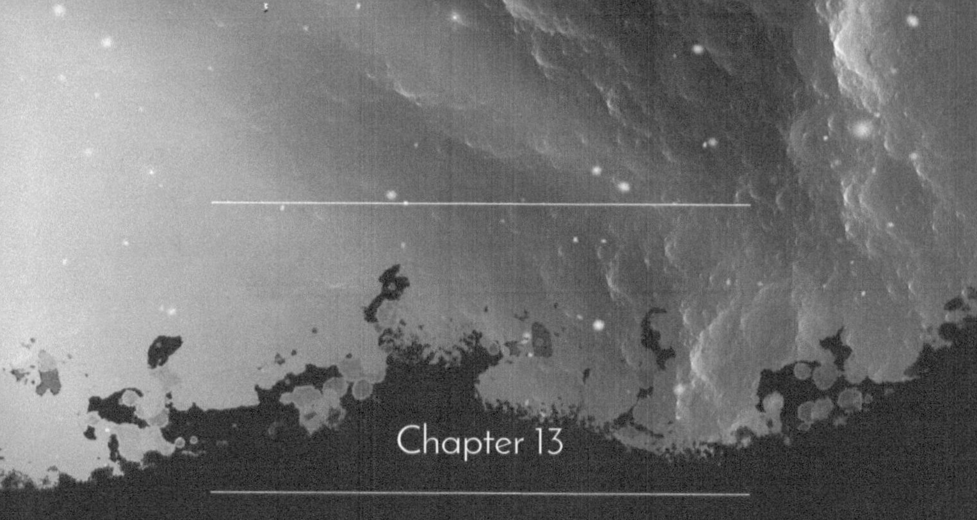

Chapter 13

"I thought we got rid of her for good." Dar stood, his expression laced with animosity as his dark eyes slid down my body. The Gartian loomed over me, his alloy arm gleaming as if just polished, his fingers curled into a tight fist.

Anger boiled up in me, heating my blood. I was tired of his unwavering hatred ... tired of his constant harassment … tired of … I was just tired of it all. But my rage fizzled as exhaustion caused my knees to buckle. I sank into the empty chair, not deeming Dar with a response.

Through my lashes I scanned the crew, my mind bogged down with indecision. I was still playing the victim, and merely reacting instead of making conscious choices.

You need to truly let go of the person you were to become the person you want to be.

With clinical detachment, I considered the situation. I'd been raised a Denard, taught to hate all species except for my own. But I'd fallen in love with Maddox, a spliced human from New Earth. From my experiences with him, I'd discovered what I'd learned about the Universe was a lie, and I'd furthered my lessons with the time I'd spent on The Pittsburgh.

There, crowded around an oblong table, sat an array of species … a spliced human, a phoenix, two Mazatimzs, a Galvraron, a spliced Talsen, a Guaviva, and a Gartian. All of them were so different, and yet … it worked. They were more than a crew; they were a family. It was something, according to what I'd been raised to believe, that should be impossible. But it wasn't. Somehow, it all worked.

Maybe the rest of the Universe had always been right about humans. They were guided by hate and prejudice, twisted by fear of the unknown. They never bothered to walk a mile in another's shoes, they simply attempted to destroy what they didn't understand, motivated by fear.

Denards are cowards. All of them.

There was no real reason for me not to get along with Dar. I could understand his blanketed dislike for the Denards—after all, they had attempted to wipe his species out of existence—but we didn't have to perpetuate a hate that had nothing to do with us. Sighing, I met Dar's gaze. "I'm sorry," I muttered. "I'm sorry for all the things I've said to you. I will do better in the future."

He stilled, surprise rolling over his features. He opened his mouth and then snapped it shut, glancing at Masha.

She nodded her head in encouragement, a silent conversation passing between them.

Dar scowled. "Words are just that. They don't mean anything without being backed by actions."

Masha's lips thinned, her eyes narrowing at him. He bowed his head, averting his gaze.

I nodded. "No, he's right. I've said a lot of things, lied more times than I can count. I have to earn all of your trust. I get it."

Jane cleared her throat. "All right. It's time to talk about what's really important—the war, or pending war, whatever it actually is. Which is part of the problem. No one seems to know what the hell is going on."

"Which is exactly what the Denards were going for, I'm sure," Zula interjected. Kade smiled indulgently at her, pulling her chair closer to his, and resting his chin on her shoulder. She shoved at him, which only made him snake his arm around her middle.

"Confusion is definitely a tactic of the Denards," Ash agreed. "I'm almost positive the attacks served as a distraction to cover up their real motives. Now all of us are scrambling to figure out what they are, stalled with indecision. Some with denial."

"Denial?" I shifted in my seat. I'd been out of the loop for such a short period of time, and yet it was as if I'd missed months' worth of intel.

"Yeah." Jane rolled her eyes. "Some species don't want to deal with the prospect of another war and they're burying their heads in the sand. They want to blame the attacks on something else, some even going as far as claiming it was a mistake."

Tamzea groaned, leaning into Eron. "The Mazatimzs won't listen to reason. Even after dealing with Xia and Tia, they can't wrap their brains around the truth."

Zula nodded. "I'm not surprised. Your people are a species of peace, healers through and through. Even when faced with what was done to you and Eron, and Xia and Tia, they want to believe it was all a mistake. A science experiment that was plotted with good intentions simply gone horribly wrong. They don't want to make a choice that goes against their nature."

"It's a shame they feel that way," I muttered. "Xia and Tia could have come in handy on our side."

Eron stood, slamming his fists against the table. "Those children have been through enough. No Mazatimz, no matter their origins, are meant to be a weapon. We are born to heal, not to do harm."

I raised my hands in defense. "Look, I'm not going to pretend to understand what it's like to be a Mazatimz. I simply was commenting on the twins being a potential asset. The more assets the better in any kind of war."

Tamzea tugged him back into his seat, her fingers running down his back. "She's not wrong."

Kade grinned, white teeth flashing in dark skin. "Ah, we don't need children when we have Talsen warriors at our disposal. In fact, we don't need anyone else besides my people."

Zula sighed, her face scrunching. "Brute force doesn't trump—"

He patted the top of her head. "Don't you worry your pretty little head, LaLa, I got this." Her cheeks heated, and she muttered under her breath. Whatever she said caused Kade's smile to brighten mischievously. It was clear he enjoyed pushing her buttons.

I glanced around the room, everyone but me talking at once. "Does anyone actually have a plan?" No one responded. I cleared my throat. "I said, does anyone have a plan?" Still no one so much as glanced my way.

Having had enough of the so-called meeting, since we were getting nowhere fast, I slunk from the room. I would take the opportunity to see Maddox while the rest of the crew was otherwise occupied.

Chapter 14

The delicate skin under Maddox's eyes was shaded with purples and blues, and his mouth hung slightly open, drool trickling from one corner. Amusement intermingled with worry. He'd been sleeping for days, literally, and he still seemed to be utterly exhausted. *Is something wrong with him?*

Approaching him slowly, I eyed the bag of fluids attached to his arm through a small tube. The presence of the small plastic bag caused my stomach to drop into my feet. Tamzea and Eron were two of the most skilled healers in Mazatimz history. If they were resorting to using such equipment and tricks, that was a damning sign about Maddox's condition.

Perching on the edge of his bed, I swept my hand across his forehead. His skin was cool and yet sweaty, clammy to the touch, and his eyes darted back and forth behind his sealed lids. I leaned into him, whispering in his ear, "Don't you dare die on me now. Not after everything I've gone through to be here."

A lump formed in my throat. There I was making it all about me again. What I'd gone through sucked, no doubt. I'd allowed myself to be tortured by my husband. But ultimately it had been my choice to accept his bad behavior. I snorted, digging my nails into my thigh. *Bad behavior. As if beating and scarring me, abusing me every day for years can be chalked up to mere bad behavior.*

Stop. Let it go. You can't change the past. There was no point in lamenting the perceived years I'd lost at the hands of Amir. Nothing I could do would ever get them back. I had to look to the future. I had to choose a new way—a better way. I would choose happiness, or at least work towards it whenever possible.

I kissed Maddox's rough cheek, inhaling his tantalizing scent. "Maddox, I don't know if you can hear me, but I love you. I've never stopped. And I want to be with you. If you can forgive me, if you can overlook all the horrible things I've done in my past, then I—" Choking back a sob, I turned away. An image of him and Cora naked and entangled skipped across my brain. I swallowed, trying again. "If you can forgive me for all the horrible things I've done, then I can forgive you for whatever you've done, too." *Even Cora.*

"Hmm, well isn't this a sticky situation." Xorik's voice swam through my mind.

I groaned. "Ah, come on. I thought you got the point and decided to leave me alone."

He chuckled, the soft sound causing all the fine hairs on my body to stand on end, and not in a pleasant way. "Some say I'm pigheaded and relentless to a fault."

"Then I'd have to agree with them." I squeezed Maddox's hand, wishing he would wake up.

"What would you give me if I could save your precious Maddox?"

My pulse sped up, my chest tightening with trepidation. "You know what's wrong with him?"

"I have my suspicions. And if I'm correct, then I'm the only one who can help him."

"No. You told me that all he needed was a healing sleep. He simply needs more time."

"I have been known to be wrong before. The fact that he hasn't awakened yet is a bad sign. You're not wrong about that. Think about it. You're already up and healed, feeling fine. He should be awake by now."

It was something I'd already been thinking. I'd recovered from what had been done to me with alarming speed. "What's wrong with him?" I squeezed his hand again, my gaze sliding over his slumbering features with fresh worry.

"How about you stop touching him and then I'll talk," Xorik snapped.

I ground my teeth together. "I'll touch him when and however I like."

"But not for long," he grated. "If you disobey me, then I won't help him."

My chest heaved as I sucked in raspy breaths, my heart

pounding out a staccato rhythm against my eardrums. Xorik's words held shades of Amir Aralias. They were controlling, and demanding, and even if Maddox wasn't in the picture … nope. Xorik threw up too many red flags for me to touch him with a twenty-foot pole. I'd done the whole possessive, controlling asshole thing, and it would never have a happy ending.

"Don't you dare think you can dictate my actions in any manner. I won't let you manipulate me. I—we don't need you. I'll find another way."

"I'll be sure to send flowers." With that Xorik was gone, his petulant tone ricocheting in my head.

There was no mistaking what he meant with the flowers comment. He seemed sure Maddox wasn't long for this mortal coil without his help.

"Fuck." I rubbed my temples, turning my gaze back to Maddox's prone form. He hadn't so much as flinched since I'd entered the room.

"My brother said he'd run some tests on him to figure out what's wrong." Zula hovered near the door. "He's the one responsible for splicing Kade. Plus, you know," she tapped the side of her head, "he is a Galvraron. We're good with figuring out seemingly unsolvable puzzles."

Hope buoyed my system. Zula's brother, Mikla, was a scientific force to be reckoned with. "He wasn't at the meeting. I thought maybe he wasn't on the ship anymore."

"No, he was busy doing who knows what. The truth is, he's bored and needs a constructive project to keep him out of trouble. Maddox is the perfect distraction.

Otherwise, Mikla might just drive everyone insane, especially me." Zula gave me a congenial smile, which seemed a bit forced.

I tugged on my hair, nerves riding me hard. I didn't know what Zula's true opinion of me was anymore. Not that it really mattered in the end. *And at least she hasn't brought up the whole crotch-sniffing incident.* "Thanks. I—"

"But he's going to need to run some tests on you as well," she interjected. "There might be a bit of pain involved." She grimaced. "Unfortunately, I've been on the receiving end of Mikla's attention before. He's a scientist before all else, and I don't have time to babysit him."

"If it'll help Maddox, I'll do anything."

Jane sidled up beside Zula. "We're going to have to tell the New Earth military something about him." She nodded in Maddox's direction. "There's a bounty on your head."

Fuckity fuck. I slapped my palm against my forehead, groaning. I'd forgotten about me abducting Maddox from Zeffrin, and leaving Cora's dead body behind. Or at least the part where I'd have to eventually deal with the consequences. "Are you planning on turning me in?" One never knew with Jane.

"No. I'm thinking you'll end up being more useful here than swinging from a noose on New Earth. They'd string you up first and ask questions later."

Zula frowned. "I wasn't aware that New Earth used antiquated forms of execution such as hanging. How barbaric. Isn't it—"

Jane smirked, slapping her on the back. "It's an expression, Smurfette. New Earth doesn't still hang people. Although they might as well." She muttered the last part under her breath.

"Won't New Earth want Maddox back if you tell them he's here on The Pittsburgh?" If his superiors demanded him back, I didn't expect Jane to hold onto him for my sake. Sure they grew up together and had a history, but she'd shot him in the arm once, so there was definitely no love lost between the two.

"No," Zula replied. "Not if we inform them that something is amiss with the splicing they did and we have a Galvraron expert on the job. Although he's valuable because of what they made him, it doesn't mean they want to expend time or resources when they don't have to."

Shifting from foot to foot, nerves pinged, causing my belly to cramp. "What they made him? What exactly were they going for with the Lunin DNA splice?"

Jane raised her hand in the air, dancing around demonstratively. "Oh! Me! Me! I know this one! New Earth contacted us when you and him went missing. They wanted to make sure we knew how important he was since he's the Alpha of his little spliced pack."

I scrubbed a hand down his face, thinking back to the team he commanded. It all made sense the way they'd reacted to him. They were just like the Lunins, and yet … "If he's an Alpha, then how did Xorik overpower him so easily? He forced a shift simply by commanding it."

Zula cleared her throat. "The Lunin Alpha from the

ship, the one Jane ran into, was born, not simply spliced. It would be like Jane going up against Ash. He would—"

Jane glowered. "You better watch what you say, Smurfette."

Zula rolled her eyes, slipping out from under her arm. "Please. We all know Ash is more powerful than you. Or are we not allowed to speak of the dark times when you were tracking him and he played you for a fool over and over again?"

"So what does that mean? Maddox is an Alpha but not as powerful an Alpha? And what about me? Where does that put me in the Lunin hierarchy?"

Mikla glided into the room, a small metallic case tucked under his arm. His lips curled up at the edges as his cold gaze roamed over me with interest. "Where do you fit in? Well, that's what I'm here to find out."

Zula poked her brother in the chest. "Maddox first, Mikla. You figure out what's wrong with him and how to fix it before you put Nina under a microscope."

He turned away from her, mumbling under his breath.

"What did you say?" she demanded.

He slammed a needle down on the table, glaring at her. "I said that I'm going to need to study her as a baseline. Therefore, I need to put her under a microscope to figure out what's wrong with Maddox. Her blood anyhow."

Jane stepped between the siblings, her hands raised. "All right. That's enough. Mikla knows better than to do something stupid and against my wishes because I'm the captain of this ship and his big brain has already come to the conclusion that I'd drop him off at the closest prison planet so fast his—"

"Fine," Mikla spat. "You don't have to threaten me … again. I'll do what Zula asked." His lower lip stuck out partway in something akin to a pout.

Flames danced in Jane's eyes. "I'll leave you to it then." She grabbed Zula's arm and pulled her towards the door.

"Jane," I said.

She paused, glancing over her shoulder.

"Thanks. For helping him … and me. Us, really."

She shrugged and cleared her throat. "You did save my life." Zula sputtered a protest as she was yanked around the corner.

I stared at the space where Jane and Zula had just been, lost in thought. Jane was well aware that I'd saved her on the diplomatic cruiser only because it'd been part of a bigger plan set up by my husband. It was how I'd come to be on The Pittsburgh as a spy. I had to gain their trust first. The fact that she'd booted me from her ship to be with Maddox, and then come to my rescue, pointed to the fact that she didn't hate me as much as she wanted me to believe.

I smiled. Maybe one day we could be friends.

Chapter 15

"So what do you want me to do?" I asked Mikla.

He glanced up at me as if surprised I'd had the nerve to speak to him. Without responding, he returned his attention to the table in front of him as he arranged his tools.

Sighing, I perched on the bed beside Maddox, taking his hand within mine. "You're going to be fine. Do you hear me? We're going to fix you without Xorik's help."

"Stop talking. It's annoying," Mikla snapped.

I bit my tongue, swallowing back a growl. *Don't antagonize the scientist who's going to fix Maddox. He simply has no bedside manner because he's not a doctor or healer.* I forced myself to take in deep normal breaths. *Good. See, that's better. You can do this. No matter how rude he is, it's better than dealing with Xorik.*

Mikla grabbed my arm, his blue-tinged fingers cold against my heated flesh. Jabbing a needle in my arm, he withdrew a small vial of blood, the metallic scent sharp. He held the sample up to the light, clucking his tongue. Rubbing the puncture wound, I glared up at him. *Asshat.* The tiny hole closed a moment later, the physical sting gone, the emotional insult continuing to burn. *Huh. Guess I heal faster now.* The rumors about that part of a werewolf must be true. I wasn't sure how I felt about that though.

Producing another needle, he proceeded to extract blood from Maddox in the same manner, lifting it up to the light when finished as well. Holding my breath, I watched Mikla's face for clues, but got none.

Labeling both vials, Mikla placed them into a small machine that began whirling around. The motion only lasted a few seconds before he extracted one of the cylinders, and tipped a smidgen onto what appeared to be a slide. He did the same with the second vial, but this time, just the one drop of blood filled my nostrils with an acrid scent, causing me to gag.

Mikla lifted his head, studying me. "Interesting. You had no reaction to your own blood, but a negative response to the smell of Maddox's. Come here." He waved me over.

I shuffled over to stand next to him. "Okay. What do you want me to do?"

"Smell each slide and tell me what your impressions are."

Raising my eyebrows, I bent to do as he asked. After all, he was the supposed genius in the room. I sniffed both slides, recoiling from the one on the right. There was something sickly sweet about it that made the scent all wrong. I didn't know exactly why I thought it, but something in me screamed in panic. *Wrong, wrong, wrong.*

I shoved my nose into the crook of my arm. "The one on the right smells wrong. I'm not exactly sure why, but my gut says it's not right. It has this sickly-sweet smell to it."

The corner of Mikla's mouth curled. "Sickly sweet in what manner? Can you expound upon that?" Lifting the slide, he waved it in front of my arm. "Smell it again."

Lowering my arm, I closed my eyes, inhaling. I forced my gag reflex to heel, concentrating on the scents hiding in Maddox's blood. "It smells like lavender, pear, with an undercurrent of bitterness," I sucked in another lungful of the foul air, "bitter almonds. Yes, lavender, pear, and bitter almonds." Having had enough, I staggered back, covering my face once again.

Mikla's eyes danced with barely contained glee. "Poison. He's been poisoned with some kind of mixture —I'm guessing synthetic. I'm also guessing … Yes, yes, yes. That Lunin nose of yours is quite talented." Whirling around, he dropped the slide onto the table and raced around the infirmary, searching for something.

My heart thrashed against my ribcage, my vision wavering. *Poison?* Maddox had some kind of poison in his bloodstream? Which meant, instead of a healing sleep, he was slowly dying. Staggering, I caught myself on the edge of his bed. *It had to be Xorik. There's no other explanation.*

"How's it going in here?" Tamzea's soft voice drew my attention.

"You knew it was poison?"

Her lavender eyes darkened. "Yes, but we weren't able to figure out what kind. The best we could do was purge his system. But when we did that it only seemed to make him worse. It's when we decided to turn to Zula and Mikla. I was afraid of making Maddox worse. Something just isn't right about him."

"I'd say so since he's been poisoned."

"No." Tamzea slid in to sit beside me, rubbing small circles along my back. Normally such physical contact would have made me balk since I wasn't used to it, but coming from a healer such as her, it had the desired soothing effect. "That's not what I mean. There's something unusual about the poison. It's also why we didn't tell Mikla what we knew. Or what we thought we knew. We wanted him to go into the situation not knowing so he—"

"Could reach his own conclusions without letting your diagnosis sway him in any way. In case you were wrong," I finished for her.

She nodded. "Exactly."

Mikla regarded Tamzea with surprise. "How very scientific of you and Eron."

She blushed. "Well, it was Zula's idea."

"Oh, then I'm not surprised. She still has her moments of clarity," he sniffed, "even though she mated with that—that thing."

Shifting, I focused on Maddox, my stomach churning with bile. "Will you be able to fix him?" *God, please, no. I can't lose him. I can't. I can't. I can't.*

Ressi popped up in front of me, her whiskers and tail twitching. "That's it. I'm hacking into that stupid Lunin ship and taking control. Even though I don't like Maddox, and think you're too good for him … well, I'm not going to let another asshole take control of your life in any way. If Xorik did this to Maddox because he's a sick, twisted stalker then I'm going to find out and I'm going to make him pay."

"Since when can you hack a ship and take control?" I demanded. It would have been nice to know before that she was capable of that. It would have saved me from a lot of issues, Xorik being one.

Her ears flattened. "Okay, I've never actually done it. But … well, I'm going to figure it out." In a huff, she disappeared.

Mikla hovered in the middle of the room, his expression contemplative as he stared at the empty space where Ressi had just been. "Your A.I. seems to be operating outside of its parameters. It was as if she was actually angry."

"Yeah, well, she's out of control. She keeps updating and changing her programs."

He grunted, turning away to scoop up something small and metallic from his workstation. "Despite the name, A.I.s are not supposed to have self-awareness. It would be dangerous. But it seems as though she does." He scratched his head. "I'd like to study her when I'm done with Maddox."

I slapped my hand over my wristband. There was no way in hell I was letting the creepy Galvraron get his hands on Ressi. Sure, he was right, her being self-aware was absolutely dangerous, particularly to my sanity, but I could never risk losing her. "Umm ... no. That's okay."

"It would be no trouble at all."

Shifting, I put my hand behind my back. "Let's just deal with Maddox first."

He frowned. "Right. It shouldn't take me very long to figure out what the poison is."

Tamzea squeezed my arm. "And then he'll be able to find a way to combat it, right, Mikla?"

He nodded absently. "If anyone can, it will be me who finds the antidote, yes."

She sighed heavily. "You're supposed to be encouraging."

He clicked his tongue several times, glaring down at his feet. "I won't lie. And I don't care whose feelings I hurt. I will do the job out of scientific curiosity, and because my sister is on a power trip and threatening to leave me stranded on a prison planet." The tips of his ears turned purple. "Because of those things, I will do my best, which is better than anyone else's." He cleared his throat and whirled back around to face his workstation, his lab coat swirling with him in a rather dramatic fashion.

Tamzea leaned in to whisper in my ear, "He'll figure it out." She glanced at Maddox. "You staying with him?"

My gaze lovingly danced over his prone form, a part of me expecting his eyes to pop open, despite the circumstances. "Yes."

Nodding once, she stood. "I'll be back soon. I have some things to take care of." She strode from the room, sparing one last glance at Mikla, a scowl forming.

A sudden yawn cracked my jaw. Curling up against Maddox's side, my eyes slid shut, heavy from exhaustion. "Wake me up if you need my help with anything else."

Before Mikla could respond in any way, I was tugged into oblivion.

Chapter 16

"Hey," Maddox rumbled, his voice ladened with sleep. Callused fingers slipped down my bare stomach, causing butterflies to dive bomb. "I half expected you to be gone when I woke up. Being with you is like a dream."

Rolling over within the circle of his strong arms, I blinked his strong features into focus. "I wish I could stay here with you forever."

His supple lips brushed against the tip of my nose. "So do it. Come with me. I could make you happy, Nina. I want to wake up to you every day. I know—"

Crushing my mouth to his, I swept my tongue in to entangle with his, effectively stealing his words. I'd met with Maddox only a handful of times now, but each time was more difficult than the last to leave him. When I was lost in his embrace, I felt so alive—vibrant. But I couldn't imagine a future with him, not really. He was everything I'd been raised to hate. I couldn't leave my family and my people behind for one man. And because of who my parents were, there'd be a price put on his head, I had no doubt.

He pulled away from me, frowning. "Why does that feel like a good-bye kiss?"

Tears burned the corners of my eyes, spilling down my temples and running into my hair. "Because it is. Good-bye, I mean. I can't see you anymore, Maddox. It's too dangerous."

His eyes clouded over. "No. You've said that before and yet every time—"

"It's different now. My mother found out about us." Rolling onto my side, I curled into a ball. "She made it painfully clear that I have to end it with you. She's forcing my hand."

"Your mother knows? Shit." He pulled me against him, the heat from his chest suffusing through my back. "She knows you're here now?"

I shook my head, sniffling. "Yes. Or well, not exactly. She gave me a week to end things with you or she said she was going to my father."

His hand clenched against my hip. "We could still run away. You'd be protected as a New Earth citizen." He flipped me onto my back, his gaze boring into mine as he pressed me into the bed. "Marry me, Nina. Marry me and we can be together for real. No more sneaking around. No more—"

I cupped his cheek, his scruff abrading my palm. "You know I can't do that. I—"

"You can. You just don't want to," he snarled, turning away from me. "So that's it? It's over? Just like that?" His voice cracked.

A guttural sob tore from my chest. "Not just like that. You know I love you. You know I—"

Stumbling to his feet, he yanked his clothes on with jerky movements. "If you loved me like you claim, you wouldn't give me up so easily."

"It's not easy! None of this is easy!"

"That's where you're wrong. It was easy for me to love you. And now that I know the truth ... it's going to be easy to walk away from you."

Jolting awake, I sat straight up, tumbling to the floor. It took a moment for my sleep-disorientated brain to come back online, and I remembered where I was. Groaning, I glanced around the infirmary, surprised to discover I was alone with Maddox.

Lurching to my feet, I made myself comfortable on the edge of Maddox's bed. I brushed my hands through his hair, the buzz cut he normally wore growing out with excessive speed. His face wasn't merely covered in stubble anymore either, but with a full beard, dark and lush. I tugged my hands through it, wondering if he would want me to shave it off.

His hand shot up to wrap around my wrist. Gasping, I lifted my gaze just as his eyes fluttered open. "Hey, now. It's not polite to tug on a man's beard when he's trying to sleep." His dark chocolate eyes sparked with gold, his lips tipping up.

"Oh my God! Maddox! You're awake!" I threw myself at him, burying my nose in his neck, inhaling his tantalizing scent.

His arm snaked around my waist, holding me firmly against him. "Yeah, I was awake long enough before for Mikla to inform me that he'd saved my life." He chuckled. "If it wasn't for the whole saving my life thing, I might have punched him. He has a serious attitude problem."

I shoved my arms underneath him in a desperate attempt to get closer. I hadn't let myself believe it until that moment, but a part of me had already been saying good-bye to him again. It's why I'd had the dream. My subconscious was preparing me for the worst. It was preparing me for the end.

Maddox tugged me up higher on his chest, my legs straddling him automatically. My fingers slid out from under him, and curled against his bare torso, my insides twisting with sudden lust. *Stop it. He just woke up after nearly dying. It isn't the time or place.* Too bad my body disagreed.

Grinning, Maddox's hands ran down my back, settling on my ass. Underneath me his cock swelled, causing a fresh surge of lust to burn through my veins. "Hell of a way to wake up." He thrust his pelvis, grinding against me.

"Maddox," I chastised, "you almost died."

"Can't think of a better way to celebrate life. Can you?"

Joy exploded within me, but I couldn't shake the niggling questions about … well, everything. Before we'd been pulled in by the Lunins, and before Xorik had forced his change and he'd fallen ill—from an unknown poison that I had no idea where it came from—Maddox hadn't wanted me. He'd made it painfully clear that his New

Earth military position was the only thing that mattered to him anymore. *And then he wakes up and is acting like everything is fine between us. Like we haven't lost years ...*

Even though he'd confessed love less than twenty-four hours ago, it'd been different and under extenuating circumstances. He'd been dying and I was pretty sure he'd been delirious to boot. *Ugh. What's going on? I want to believe him, to simply go with the flow of his emotions, but I can't trust it. Any of it. But dear God, I want to ... so desperately.*

Pain shot through my skull, and I doubled over. "Hands off. He can't have what's mine."

"Nina, what's wrong?" Maddox cradled me to him, smoothing my hair back from my face.

"Xorik," I gritted out between clenched teeth. "He's in my head. Trying to keep me from touching you. He wants—"

"I know what he wants," Maddox snarled. "And he can't have it. Do you hear me, Xorik? Nina's mine."

A dark laugh swirled through my head. "Tell the pup that he snoozed and he lost. He should have claimed you when he had the chance."

"I'm not anyone's to claim. I make my own decisions, my own choices, and I decide who I'm going to be with." Surging up, I let instinct guide me. Fangs sprouted, long and sharp, and without thought I plunged them into Maddox's neck, snarling against his flesh.

He tipped his head back, a moan morphing into a howl as he clawed my back. Undulating against him, I tore at his clothes, needing him to be inside of me more than my next breath. Fabric tore and buttons popped, cool air causing goose bumps to skitter over my skin.

And then bliss.

Euphoria.

Ecstasy.

Maddox's thick cock filled me up, wrenching pleasure from me as my body took the same from him. We rutted against each other, like the two wild animals we were, not caring about anything in that moment besides each other.

"Fuck, fuck … fuck," Maddox growled, pulsating his release into me, just as I quivered around him. "Neens … fuuuuck."

Grabbing his hair, I yanked his face towards mine, fusing our lips together. I wanted more. Much more. Infinitely more. And I was going to have it. We had years to make up for. So many lost years.

Sliding off of him, I strutted across the room, smiling when Maddox's golden eyes glazed over as they followed my every move. I leaned over a nearby cot, wriggling my ass at him.

His jaw slack, Maddox ran a hand down his face, a low growl rumbling in his chest. Jumping to his feet, his cock bobbed, already rock hard again. He cupped the side of his neck where I'd bitten him. "Do you even know what you did?"

"Yeah, I bit you—marked you as mine." It wasn't the same kind of bite Xorik had given me. That one had served a different purpose. The bite I'd given Maddox, it was something I'd known to do on instinct. He was mine, and I'd claimed him. Now every other Lunin would know it, too.

"My turn."

Squealing with delight, I bucked as Maddox plunged into me from behind, his claws raking down my hips. I no longer cared what had changed to make him want me again, all that mattered was that he did, and he was about to claim me just like I'd done to him.

His teeth and fangs scraped along my neck as if savoring the moment leading up to what I now considered the inevitable. When the sharp points sank into my flesh, finding their home, I moaned long and loud, falling off into another orgasm.

"I've thought about nothing else since the moment I was turned," he groaned, his tongue laving against my flesh. "I never stopped," his pace turned brutal, his hips pistoning against my ass, "never stopped. Fuuuuck," he rasped. "Fuck. So good."

He slumped along my back, his hot flesh still pulsing within me, our sweat-slicked skin sticking together.

Is this real? Is any of this real?

Yes. It is. Leave the past behind. You deserve good things, too. You deserve them because you'll do all the things to make that your new reality. Choose happiness. I'd decided my new life was about me always having the choice, and I chose Maddox. I wouldn't accept any more excuses, from myself or him. The rest was simply background noise.

Chapter 17

"Blind! Blind! I'm blind!" Jane's agitated voice dragged me from sleep. "I can't unsee what I've just seen! I can't even walk around my own damn ship without stumbling across someone's naked ass."

"I never hear you complain when it's my naked ass you're stumbling across," Ash retorted, mirth in his tone.

"Yeah, well that's different. Your ass is a work of art. I could stare at it all damn day."

My eyes fluttered open, the underside of Maddox's chin, mostly his beard, taking up the entirety of my view. Wiggling, I realized I was splayed across his chest, yep … naked. *Shit. It's my ass Jane is talking about.* I sat up, realizing we hadn't even made it back to the cot. Instead, we'd passed out on the floor right next to it.

A folded sheet flopped to the floor in front of me. "Cover up, damnit," Jane growled.

My cheeks heated, and I scrambled to pull the sheet over us. The scratchy material slid along my skin, causing me to shiver. "Sorry," I muttered.

Maddox yawned and stretched, settling his hands under his head. "Calm down, Jane. It's not like we have anything you haven't seen before."

"That's not the point."

I leaned into him, hissing under my breath, "I don't want anyone seeing you naked but me. Especially not your ex-girlfriend."

"Jane has me now," Ash interjected. The rest was left unsaid. Although Ash was the opposite of jealous, smug about his prowess to a fault, I supposed even he couldn't resist commenting on Maddox's nudity. After all, Jane and Maddox had been a couple back when they were teenagers on New Earth. There were no lingering feelings beyond friendship, and Ash knew it, but the male ego was a strange thing.

"Was there something you wanted?" Maddox asked, his gaze dropping to fixate on the swell of my breasts.

Jane cleared her throat. "Umm, yeah. Not that I need a reason to go into any part of *my* ship, but … Mikla told us the antidote he gave you should have you feeling as good as new and we came to check in on things."

"As you can see, Mikla was quite right. Good as new." Maddox's eyes twinkled as they met mine.

"Obviously," Ash drawled.

Maddox's expression dropped into hard lines, the muscles in his jaw popping. "Did Mikla figure out what kind of poison was in my system and how it was administered?"

Jane tightened the ponytail in her hair and shifted. "He's still working on that, but Tamzea made him move to another room. She thought all the noise he was making could disturb you two." She smirked. "Probably would have been the other way around."

"Because Jane gets distracted so easily, I thought I'd mention the actual reason we came down here, besides checking on you."

Jane elbowed Ash in his ribs. "Hey. I do not get distracted easily." His eyebrows lifted, and she scowled as if her menacing facial expression could make him change his mind.

"As I was saying, because Jane gets so easily distracted, I thought I'd let you know that we're stopping at a supply space station soon. We need to pick up a few things that can't wait. We want everyone to be ready for whatever we might find there. We have no idea what to expect."

"How soon?" I asked.

Jane glanced at the door, shifting from foot to foot. "Zula was deciding which one in the area would be the safest. So it could be any time now. She'll let everyone know over the intercom," she narrowed her eyes at me, "so don't go yanking yours out of the wall again."

I raised my hands in the air, the sheet sliding off my breasts. "That was one time. And it was because of—" I pulled the sheet back up to cover me. "Oops, sorry. As I was saying—"

"Don't care." Jane waved her hand at me as she turned to leave. "There's no excuse for you to do anything to my ship without my permission. Just remember that for future reference."

"Noted," I mumbled.

Maddox's hands slid into my hair, capturing my full attention. "All of this seems like a dream."

I smiled. "I know exactly what you mean." My stomach flip-flopped. And that was the thing about dreams, eventually, you had to wake up. I nibbled on my bottom lip, wanting to talk to Maddox about … well, everything. We had so much to discuss, but I wasn't ready to pop our happy little bubble yet.

His callused index finger pressed between my eyebrows, smoothing out the pucker there, before following the line of one of my scars. Averting my gaze, I snatched at his wrist. "Stop. Don't touch them. I don't want to be reminded." I swallowed the glass shards in my throat. "For the first time, when I was with you, I forgot. I almost forgot."

He cupped my face, forcing me to meet his gaze. "We have a lot to talk about, things that need to be said before we can actually put the past behind us." He brushed his full lips against mine, his beard tickling me. "But in the meantime, don't think for one second that a couple of scars makes you any less beautiful to me."

"But when you first saw them, you could barely look at me. I know—"

"It wasn't the scars that horrified me. It was what you

must have gone through to get them … I hated myself for not being able to protect you. I never should have let you go."

"No. It wasn't your place to protect me. Although I won't lie and deny the fact that I used to wish you'd come for me, even when I knew you never would."

His hands dropped away from me, and he tucked his chin against his chest. "Fuck. I would have. If I had known what he was doing to you all those years I would have murdered him with my bare hands. I blame myself for—"

"No. The only one to blame is me. I made the choice to break things off with you. I made the choice to let my mother bully me into marrying someone else. I made the choice to stay … and to be the victim. All the horrible things I've done have been my choice. And I take full responsibility for them. All of them."

"Neens, baby, it wasn't your choice to be treated like that. It wasn't—"

"Yes, it was," I croaked. "I could have done so many things differently. I made all the wrong choices, the biggest one being that I convinced myself that I was trapped without any options. It broke me. Shattered me to oblivion." My chest tightened, and my skin heated. "And there was no one there to help pick up the pieces. I chose to let myself be isolated. But then … then something changed. Something clicked into place. I don't feel like the same person anymore, Maddox." I attempted to smile but wasn't sure if the muscles in my face responded. "And I'm glad for it."

His lips smashed into mine, the kiss one of support and love. It said everything that Maddox couldn't, or didn't want to put into words, and I silently thanked him by losing myself in him. Our bodies communicated the loss of us being separated, the devastation and pain, all of it being wiped away with the culmination of finding each other again. It was the simplest of dances, but the most beautiful in existence, because it was one of understanding and complete acceptance.

I still had so many questions, some that needed answers, and others I was willing to let go. The Universe was in turmoil, utter chaos threatening to destroy all of us ... which was why we had to savor each perfect moment before it slipped away. For there was no way to tell if it would be the first of many, or the last. Nothing in life is guaranteed, and all we can do is decide to make the best out of the time we do have.

Chapter 18

"I'm going to have to go back. They need me. New Earth needs me." Maddox pulled a beige T-shirt over his head and stood.

Lounging on my bed, I jutted my lower lip out in a mock pout. "It's a shame to cover up abs like yours."

He frowned, although his eyes twinkled, roaming down my bare flesh. "You're avoiding the topic at hand. I have to go back to my unit, and I want you to come with me."

Poof. Happy bubble officially gone. Hello, reality. Shifting up onto my elbows, I regarded him solemnly. "And what do you expect me to do? Join your little unit as one of your wolfy soldiers?"

He snorted. "No, of course not. I'd expect you to wait for me on New Earth safe and sound, away from the fighting."

My jaw slackened. *He can't be fucking serious. He has to be joking.* "Umm ... I'm not even a New Earth citizen."

Leaning into the oblong mirror on the wall, he tugged at his beard. "Not yet you aren't, but once we get married it won't be a problem. I'll make a special request to have the license pushed through. We can—"

Left hand on my hip, I waggled my right hand at him. "Nope. I don't think so." I strode towards him, not caring that I was still naked. "You're not just going to tuck me away on New Earth and expect me to wait for you." Poking him in the back with my index finger, I scowled at his reflection in the mirror. "If that's what you want, then I'll stay here and help Jane. This is my war just as much as it is yours."

His lip curled. "As of right now, there isn't much of a war going on. I'd feel better knowing you were safe and sound on New Earth so I didn't have to worry about you. Do you want me to constantly be worrying about you getting into who knows what kind of trouble with Jane?"

I shoved at him, hating how my nipples tightened when his gaze tracked down to watch my breasts jiggle. "Eyes up here, asshat. You don't get to ogle the goods while we're having a fight."

"What?" he muttered.

"I said," shoving at him again, claws sprouting from my fingertips, "no ogling the goods when we're fighting."

"Then put on some damn clothes if you don't want me to look. Or is that your strategy? Huh? You going to jiggle me into submission?"

I tightened my scowl, trying not to laugh. "Jiggle you into submission? What the fuck?"

He spun around, cupping my breasts roughly. "These. You keep jiggling them in my face and I can't think about anything else."

"Not my fault you're easily—"

He dipped his head, capturing my right nipple within his mouth.

"Not fair," I muttered, anger instantly morphing into red-hot lust.

He broke away from me long enough to wink. "If you're not going to fight fair then neither am I."

"EVERYBODY GET their asses up here now, we're about to dock," Jane's voice boomed over the intercom. "No exceptions. Chop, chop."

My gaze slid up to Maddox, who was grinding his teeth in response to Jane. "She doesn't get to boss me around. I'm not a member of her crew."

"Was she always like that? Even back when you were teenagers?"

"No." He bent over to retrieve his clothes, which I'd shed him of again. "But there were signs."

I perched my chin on my hand, watching as he covered all of his delectable skin in drab colors. "Signs?"

"Yeah, definite red flags. Like when she shot me when I broke things off with her."

Scooting out of bed, I searched the floor for my own discarded clothes. "Why did she shoot you? I mean, she never seemed to be hung up on you."

He grunted. "Bad timing, I guess. I didn't know her parents had just kicked her out of their house and she was counting on me for support. I would have offered her a place to stay if she would have talked to me instead of flying off the handle."

"She didn't say anything to you?"

He tugged on his boots. "No. I broke it off with her after our test results because I knew we wouldn't see much of each other anymore. Plus, we were both messes back then. I couldn't take care of myself let alone her. I mean, I loved her, but I realized I wasn't in love with her. She didn't figure that out until later."

I nodded. The fact that neither of them had been in love was why their relationship didn't bother me. Anyone who knew Jane and Maddox could see that the two of them wouldn't make a good couple. At least not long term.

"Did you— Have you—" I swallowed my words. It didn't matter. I didn't need to ask. Maddox had told me that I was the only woman in his heart. It didn't matter if he'd said it while he was delirious. I knew it was true. I wasn't about to be needy. "Never mind." I plastered a smile on my face.

Maddox grabbed my arm, my boot falling from my hand. "In case you need to hear it again. I love you, Neens, so much. You're the only woman who's ever been in my heart. When I let you walk away you took a piece of me with you."

"Cora …" Her name tumbled from my mouth, and I grimaced. I told myself I'd let it go. All of it. And yet there I was bringing it up anyways.

He sighed, his thumb sweeping over the sensitive skin on the inside of my wrist. "This is the only time I'm going to say this. I'll lay all my cards on the table, but then we're moving on. Do you hear me?"

I nodded vigorously. "Of course. I want to move on. I do."

"All right, I get it. Knowing about it is some kind of closure." He expelled another long breath, his shoulders slumping. "I've only ever loved you, Nina, but after you … yeah, okay, after you, I fucked a lot of women. But it was just sex. I never felt anything for any of them beyond mild affection. I cared about Cora because she was one of my soldiers. But she was a mistake. A big mistake." He tugged at his beard. "Because of what we are, she got it in her head that she wanted me for her mate. I didn't realize it until you showed up. Guess she didn't feel like she had any competition besides you, and that eventually I'd see things her way."

Don't ask … don't ask … don't ask … You don't need to know. Seriously, there is no purpose in knowing. "How many is a lot?" *Damn it. Why can't I keep my mouth shut even when I want to? Oh, well, too late now.*

Maddox barked out a humorless laugh. "Nope. Not going there. The number doesn't matter."

My nostrils flared, sudden agitation tightening my chest as I struggled to breathe normally. "Am I going to be running into your conquests everywhere I turn? Just give me a number so I'm prepared."

"Nina," he growled, "no. This conversation, if we continue it, is not going to end well for either of us."

"You know my number."

"That's because it's two."

I ground my teeth together. "It doesn't matter. You know mine, and I want to know yours."

"What the hell is taking everyone so long to get up here?" Jane's voice crackled over the intercom. "I said no exceptions, and here I am, alone. All of you get your asses up here, now! That's an order from your captain!"

"What am I, invisible?" Ash's voice could be heard before Jane switched off the intercom.

Grabbing my hand, Maddox tugged me out into the hallway. I trudged along behind him, shooting daggers from my eyes at his back.

"You will tell me your number," I proclaimed. "I'm not letting it go."

Maddox mumbled under his breath and shook his head.

I retracted my hand from his. "What? I couldn't hear you. You're going to have to speak up."

He glared at me over his shoulder. "I was just saying that you might be more demanding than Jane. And that gives me pause. You're not planning on shooting me, are you?"

I bared my teeth. "Not if you tell me your number."

He quickened his pace. "I'm not going to fight with you, Neens. Not about this. Just accept that I love you and that I'm not going to fuck anyone else ever again."

"I love you, too, asshat! Which is why I want to know," I called after him, his muscular form disappearing around the corner. The jackass couldn't get away from me fast enough. Maybe I would have to shoot him just to slow him down.

Tamzea appeared beside me out of nowhere, causing my heart to quadruple in time. She smiled as I attempted to catch my breath. "Men are complicated creatures."

Eron fell into step beside her, snorting derisively. "No, we're not."

Tamzea and I locked gazes, sudden laughter overtaking us as we said in unison, "No, they're not."

Chapter 19

Despite the political climate that had brokered war, I was the happiest I'd been in years, maybe ever. Not only had I found my way back to Maddox, but there was a tentative acceptance of me among the crew of The Pittsburgh. Even Dar was regarding me warily, instead of with his usual outright hatred. It gave me hope for a future. One that I would fight for with my dying breath. It was better to fight for something, to reach and strive for a positive, than to drown in a negative such as revenge. I by no means had forgiven the Denards, or my family for that matter, but I wasn't going to destroy myself in an attempt to destroy them as well.

"What's all of this?" Maddox demanded, his eyes roaming over the weapons strewn about on the floor just beyond the airlock. Jane herself had an arsenal strapped to her legs, arms, and back. It was amazing that she was able to stand up straight under the weight of it all.

Removing a laser handgun from her thigh, Jane tossed it on the ground and picked up a slightly bigger gun. She grinned. "Oh, didn't I tell you? We might have to shoot our way in … and out of the supply space station. We're all going in."

Glancing around at the rest of the crew, I noticed that none of them seemed any more pleased than I was.

Masha peered out from behind Dar, her large, black eyes welling with tears. "But who will watch my engine?"

Tamzea paled. "Shoot? As in shoot people? Jane, you know I'm not good with blood unless I'm healing someone."

Kade shoved Zula behind him, scowling as his eyes lit up like two yellow flashlights. "I'd rather Zula stay here on the ship where I know she'll be safe."

Maddox nodded. "I'm with Kade. I don't want Nina going out there."

Jane laughed. "I was joking. I don't need all of you. Just you," she pointed at me, and then her index finger moved in Maddox's direction. "and you. The rest of you have jobs to do here."

Maddox growled, "And why do you need Nina? I'm more than happy to go with you and Ash. But she's—"

I shoved at Maddox, causing him to stumble to the right, knocking him into Kade. The Talsen warrior caught him, eyeing me with a smirk. "You don't get to decide what I do or don't do. I'm not fully human anymore, remember? I can hold my own in a fight now." I could hold my own in a fight before, but I knew being a Class 1, which was what my human status had translated to, made weapons necessary. Now, with claws, fangs, heightened senses, and accelerated healing capabilities, I was a force to be reckoned with.

"Yeah, okay," Maddox tugged at his beard, "you go through the change and boom, you can kick everyone's ass. That's not how it works. If you don't know how to control yourself, your Lunin blood can actually put you more at risk. I trained for months before they let me out of my cage."

Tilting my head, I quirked an eyebrow. "But you were spliced. I was made. How I feel now is … natural, like second nature. It's who I am. I don't need to train."

Maddox's fist met the wall behind him with a dull thud. "Would you please, for the love of God, woman, just do what I say for once?"

I sympathized with Maddox, really I did. I knew compromise was a part of any healthy relationship. But some things were nonnegotiable. I bit my lower lip and batted my eyelashes. "Oh, but I did do what you wanted, over and over again when we were naked. Isn't that good enough for you? Because if it isn't, I can always—"

"You're driving me insane. I need to keep you safe. Please, Neens, just stay on the goddamn ship."

"It's probably the wolf in you," Kade interjected. "I bet

it rides you hard just like the dragon in me. I have to watch over Zula constantly."

Zula narrowed her eyes at him. "Not constantly. Not anymore. Right?"

Kade dipped his head, the dark curtain of his hair falling down to block his face. "I can't help it. It makes me feel better."

She smacked his arm. "We're together—mated. You can't continue to let the irrational part of you override logic. You stalking me doesn't help anything."

Pushing his hair behind his ears, Kade grinned. "It helps me."

"Oh, you're infuriating." Zula whirled around, crossing her arms over her chest.

Maddox leaned into me, his hot breath tickling my ear. My stomach clenched with want as his delicious scent surrounded me. "At least I don't stalk you."

My lips twitched. "Not yet."

His arms snaked around me. "I just want you to be safe."

No. Do not let his close proximity goad you into wavering in your decision. It's yours. Own it. You can't let him start manipulating you now. Sliding out of his grasp, I bent to pick up two laser guns, addressing Jane. "Which one is better?"

"Both," she said, rolling her eyes.

"Both?"

"Yeah, just take them both."

Ignoring Maddox, I armed myself with the two guns, sliding one in the back of my pants, and one in the front. "So what's the plan?"

Ash's sharp bark of laughter caused me to jump. "Plan? Jane have an actual plan? You must be joking."

"I'm going back to my engine," Masha spoke up. "I want to double-check on some things."

"Has anyone seen Mikla?" Zula asked. "I think he's hiding from me."

Kade scooped her up, tossing her over his shoulder. "Come on, LaLa, we'll find him."

Pummeling his back, she yelled, "Put me down. I'm perfectly capable of walking on my ..." Her voice faded as they rounded the corner.

I adjusted my weapons, tuning out the rest of the crew's antics. "Why do you need us to go with you at all? And what's so important that you need to get from a supply space station?"

Jane glanced at Ash and then shrugged. "I'm after information on what's going on out there in the big, wide open. I'm tired of sitting around and waiting. The Denards attacked, everyone was scrambling around to form alliances and the like, some went running for the hills, but at least it felt like everything was coming to a head. At least a war is honest. But this," she raised her arms, "it's too quiet."

"Mmm," Maddox grunted. "I agree. The attacks were a distraction, but for what?"

"Maybe it was just a test." I could feel all of their eyes burning into me. "I mean, with all the threats of an uprising of some sort, you would think the attacks would have been a catalyst. Maybe they wanted to test what would happen if they blatantly attacked. With species such as the Gartians withdrawing, who were major players from the beginning ..."

"What about the secret weapon factories stored on planets like Zeffron?" Jane demanded. "What about those?"

"Maybe they've been there for a long time, or maybe—"

"So you think it could be a test?" Ash mused, his expression turning pensive. "And then by not following up with anything, it would put people like us in a panic." He scowled. "Those sneaky bastards."

"I could be wrong though. I was merely thinking out loud. I do find it rather odd that they launched such a wide-scale massive attack and didn't follow it up with anything. Unless ..."

Maddox touched my arm. "Unless what?"

"Unless something happened within their ranks, like within their chain of command. Amir— I mean Ambassador Aralias was in charge of coordinating the Denards hidden within the UGFS. With him gone, there might have been a breakdown somewhere. The left hand may not have known what the right hand was going to do. And if that's the case—"

Maddox's forehead wrinkled. "Then all they need is

time to get things back in order. Time that we've been giving them."

"Which is why we need information," Jane interjected. "It's time to force something to happen. We can't exist like this anymore."

Silence fell over the room, each of us lost in our own thoughts. I agreed with Jane. We couldn't act without information, but I didn't think we were going to find anything useful at a supply space station.

I cleared my throat. "This isn't going to work. We need real information. Information we're not going to find here."

Jane tilted her head, adjusting a set of goggles. "What do you suggest?"

I swallowed, averting my gaze from Maddox who was trying to ensnare it with his. "I'll contact my father. Beg for him to take me in. I'll go undercover with a concocted story about what happened with Ambassador Aralias."

"No." Maddox grabbed me by the shoulders. "If you get caught they'll kill you."

"Then I just have to not get caught." Unhooking the guns from my pants, I let them clatter to the floor. "Has anyone seen my A.I.? I'm going to need her, and she's been missing since her declaration of war against Xorik."

Maddox shook me, the bitter scent of his anger reaching my nose. "You can't do this. I won't let you."

Peeling his fingers off of my shoulders, one by one, I glared up at him. "You don't get a choice. I'm the only one who can do this, and I'm going to."

It was my chance at redemption. A chance to put things right. I could learn to live with the mistakes of my past, sure, but I also needed to ensure history didn't repeat itself. I wouldn't let the Denards destroy any more lives. It was my responsibility, as someone who could, to do my best to stop them.

Chapter 20

"Maddox." I stood at the airlock, a few steps away from my destiny, as corny as that sounded. "Can't you even say good-bye?"

He hadn't said one word to me since I made my intentions to go through with my plan clear. His golden eyes merely tracked me with a brooding sullenness. Gone was the twinkle in his eyes, and the merriment in his mood. It was like he was already mourning my loss even though I was still standing right in front of him.

My heart dropped into my feet. "Fine. Be that way." I didn't expect him to rejoice at my decision, but I'd at least expected support. Not the cold indifference he was freezing me out with.

With a low growl, he ate up the distance between us, roughly grabbing the sides of my face. "I won't say good-bye because I can't—I can't even think about you not coming back. I can't think of any kind of good-bye with you ever again. Nothing is good about it."

Trembling, I bit my lower lip, tracing the lines of his face with my gaze. "Fine. Then don't say good-bye. Tell me you love me and that you'll be waiting for me."

The muscles in his jaw rippled. "I love you, Neens. And I'll always be waiting for you because we haven't had nearly enough time together." He brushed his lips against mine, inhaling sharply. "Not nearly enough."

A lump formed in my throat, my body protesting what I was about to do. It yearned to never leave his embrace, to curl up against him for the rest of eternity.

"I have to go."

His arms tightened around me to an almost painful point. "Please reconsider. Stay. Stay with me."

"I'll be back. I promise."

His nose pressed into my hair, his hot breath warming me. "Kade's right. The wolf in me is like his dragon. It gives me urges that I can't fight. It makes me want to lock you away from everyone just to make sure you're safe. Sometimes I hate that part of me … the wolf. I feel like it broke me into two people."

"It's funny how you and Kade think of the beasts in you as something separate, as a different part of you. I feel the opposite. It's as if the moment I was bitten, everything snapped into place for me. I can see things more clearly than I ever have before. I don't feel a separation of any kind. It's all just me. And for the first time in my life, it's as if I finally know who I am and what I want. Things were muddled before." I nuzzled Maddox's chest, the cotton of his shirt warm against my cheek. "As much as I hated it at first, I think … no, I know I like being what I am now."

Maddox pulled away from me, his eyes searching mine. "It must be different for someone who's been bitten versus spliced."

"That doesn't seem to be the case with Jane." I touched his face, and his eyes slid closed as he turned into my palm. "You know what I think?"

He grunted, his nose moving down to sniff the inside of my wrist.

"You and Kade haven't accepted that the beastly urges are all you. There isn't a dragon or a wolf inside of either of you. You are the wolf, and he is the dragon."

I extradited myself from Maddox, my heart clenching at the loss. We stared at each other for a moment, so much left to say, but not enough time to say any of it.

Turning away from him, I paused at the entrance to the airlock, sucking in deep, calming breaths. *I love you,* I whispered in my mind. *I'll be back. I swear it. Even if I have to haunt you.*

I wondered if there would be a time when we'd be able to communicate with our minds through our mate bond. Jane and Ash could do it, and Xorik slipped into my mind easily since he was the one who'd bitten me. But one never knew when splicing was involved.

A large hand clamped down onto my shoulder. I

gasped, my heart setting off at a gallop. My gaze swung around to find Dar standing behind me, his expression fierce.

"If you are earnest in this mission—if you succeed …" He bowed his head. "Then I will offer you my thanks." His fingers bit into my flesh. "But if this is another way of tricking us, and Masha is put in danger in any way … I'll kill you with my bare hands and no one will be able to stop me, not even Jane, or Maddox for that matter."

I swallowed audibly. "Noted. And thanks, I think." His hand fell away, and he backed up, his gaze burning into the side of my head as I stepped through the airlock.

Muscles tense, heart thrumming an erratic rhythm, I haltingly made my way down the ramp from The Pittsburgh and into the supply space station.

This is it. You can do this. You will do this.

Maddox's forlorn expression flashed in my mind, causing my gut to clench. *I won't lose you again. I refuse.*

Trudging from where the ship was docked into the main part of the station, I realized I was alone. There weren't any other beings, humanoid or other, crowding the hallways like normal. Several maintenance robots zoomed by, paying me no mind.

My boots echoed loudly on the polished metal floors, the walls gleaming as if freshly polished. UGFS-sanctioned supply space stations were all the same in their layout, so once you'd seen one, you'd seen them all in a way. My plan was to find my way to the bar, which would be tucked away in the far corner of the station, and to make contact with someone who could connect me with my family. I was going to feign ignorance of my husband's death and pretend that I thought I was still undercover on The Pittsburgh. It was a simple plan and the best that any of us could come up with.

"Nina. I need to talk to you."

Halting mid-step, I whirled around at the familiar voice, dread churning in my gut. "Johnny?"

The tall, thin, red-headed Denard, dressed in casual clothes as opposed to his usual UGFS official uniform, grabbed my arm roughly, yanking me into a dark alcove. "We've been trying to contact you. What happened?"

I widened my eyes, feigning disbelief. "What do you mean? You can't be seen with me. I'm here with The Pittsburgh. You know this."

His fingers bit into my arm. "Ambassador Aralias has been missing. We tracked The Pittsburgh here in hopes of talking to you."

My heart threatened to break free from my ribcage, sweat gathering at the base of my spine. *Shit. How were they still able to track our ship? I thought I'd removed all the trackers. I need to get word to Jane.* "What? He's missing? Since when?"

His eyes narrowed with suspicion. "Why didn't you try to contact us after the attacks? What have you been up to on The Pittsburgh?"

"Up to? You know exactly what I've been up to. And

how was I supposed to contact anyone after the attacks when I didn't know what the hell was going on? No one told me what was going to happen." I shoved at him, hissing, "I could have been killed because of it. How am I supposed to do my job and stay out of trouble if no one tells me what's coming my way?"

Johnny puffed out a breath. "When's the last time you heard from your husband?"

I shrugged. "Not sure. Where do you think he is?"

Ignoring my question, he tugged me from the alcove. "I'm bringing you in. Now."

Internally I smiled. It couldn't have been going any more perfect. I didn't even have to find someone to contact the Denards, they'd come straight to me. "No, you can't. I'm exactly where Amir wants me. I'm in a prime position to—"

"None of it matters anymore with the Ambassador missing. You can't—" Johnny's head snapped to the side, a grinding of bone and a sharp crunch just as his eyes widened for an instant before going blank. He crumpled to the ground, landing with legs and arms akimbo.

Xorik stepped over his body, a lopsided grin adorning his face. "You know you could have taken him out easily with your Lunin strength."

A low growl reverberated in my chest. "Did you stop to think that I didn't want to take him out? Huh?" Claws and fangs sprouted as I attempted to keep my temper in check. "What the hell are you doing here? I told you I want nothing to do with you." Tensing, I prepared for an epic fight. There was no way I was letting Xorik take me again. I'd kill him first, and myself for that matter.

"And what about Maddox, are you the one who poisoned him?" I'd rip out his throat with my teeth if he was the one who was responsible for Maddox nearly dying.

"Poison? What are you talking about?" His expression was open and sincere, his scent not wavering to point at a lie. Either he was the best actor I'd ever come across or he was telling the truth. *If he didn't do it, then who did?* Of course, I was new to the whole Lunin thing, and I didn't exactly have all the subtleties of sniffing out lies just yet, even though most of it seemed to be instinctual. Still, my gut said he was telling the truth.

I gnawed on the inside of my cheek. "Yeah, well I'm still not happy with you about what you just did to Johnny. I needed him alive."

He ran his hand through his hair, tilting his head. "Oops, then." He shrugged. "Sorry if I caused you any inconvenience." He motioned to Johnny's body and grimaced. "Is it a bad time to ask for a favor then?"

"A favor," I guffawed. "You are asking me for a favor?" I narrowed my eyes at him. "It better not be sexual in nature."

His goofy grin returned, and I realized he was attempting to be charming and submissive to me. "I've accepted your choice in mate. Granted, I would have fought until the last minute before the claiming, but what's done cannot be undone."

"Okay," I drawled. "Then what the hell are you doing here?"

He bowed his head. "I wish to ask for a favor, like I said."

I waved my hand at him. "All right. Spit it out. What is this so-called favor that you came all the way here to ask for instead of communicating with me in my mind."

"I didn't have a choice but to do it in person. When you mated it cut off my connection to you, unless you open up to me." He chuckled. "And I have a feeling that's not going to happen any time soon."

"You got that right, buddy." I glanced over my shoulder, my pulse pounding. It generally wasn't the brightest idea to stand around a supply space station having a casual conversation over a dead body. It was bound to cause problems for everyone involved. "Again, spit out the damn favor. I don't have all damn day."

Xorik scuffed his foot along the floor, his gaze averted. "I wish to discuss with your Maddox the possibility of Lunins finding mates among New Earth women."

"What?" *I'm having an auditory hallucination of some sort. There's no way he said what I think he just did.*

"After the ... situation with you, myself and some of the other Alphas from different tribes have decided that we can no longer wait around for mates the way we have been. And I also don't want to follow in my father's footsteps, so I—"

Raising my hand, I stopped him short. "Okay, great. I get where you're going with this but now is not the time.

I'm sure if your intentions are … pure, then some kind of arrangement can be made."

His lopsided grin reappeared, complete with tongue lolling out the side of his mouth, causing him to appear extremely wolfy. "I will help you with the body then, and afterwards we can go aboard your ship to speak with your mate."

"Whoa, whoa, whoa. I said now is not the time. We have more important things to worry about. I'm actually a bit busy at the moment."

His lips twisted down into a frown. "Our race is dying off. Time is not exactly our friend either."

"And all of us could be killed off by the Denards if you don't—"

"Nina?" I spun on my heels, coming face-to-face with another Denard in plain clothes. His gaze swung wildly down to Johnny's body, and then back up to me. "What's going on?"

Coming to a split-second decision, I opened my mouth wide and screamed. Rushing towards Silver, I grabbed onto his arm, tugging him with me as I ran. "Thank God you found me. That lunatic snapped Johnny's neck right in front of me and I was trying to convince him not to do the same to me." I picked up my pace. "Run! He could be right behind us! Run!"

Silver was young, barely out of diapers, or that's the way it seemed. He wasn't suspicious by nature, so I was hoping he'd believe my story without too much convincing on my part. "What is he? What's his class level?"

"Not sure. Don't know what he is, except strong enough to break someone's neck with his bare hands."

He nodded. "Okay. We'll get you safely on the ship, and then we'll send some people to take care of him," he swallowed, "and Johnny."

"Good. I need to talk to my husband." Since Silver didn't know what I'd spoken to Johnny about, if at all, it was best to feign ignorance on my husband missing again, so I'd have a chance to sell my obliviousness to the situation story again.

"Shit. Johnny didn't get a chance to tell you? The Ambassador—your husband is missing. It's why we tracked you."

"What? Missing? Since when?"

That's right, the tracker. I almost forgot. Opening up my mind, I reached out to Maddox. *Please work. Please work. Maddox, can you hear me?* An image of him sitting in the eating lounge with the rest of the crew on The Pittsburgh flashed across my brain, but I wasn't able to open up the connection all the way. *Shit, shit, shit. I need to let Jane know. I just need to— Xorik.*

"Xorik!" I mentally shouted. "Go to The Pittsburgh and tell Jane that the Denards have a way to track them. They tracked us here."

"Yes, I'll go." Xorik sounded eager, and I knew he'd use the excuse of sending the information as one to open up a dialogue with Maddox. It was how I knew he'd get the job done.

"Come on, Nina, this way." Silver's voice jerked me back to the task at hand, and I sprinted along beside him, shoving my nerves deep down.

This is it. This is what you wanted. The sooner you complete this mission, the sooner you can be in Maddox's arms again.

Chapter 21

Being back on my dearly departed husband's ship felt … surreal. Every nook and cranny, it seemed, held memories of countless hours spent in my own personal hell. The ship itself was an official UGFS diplomatic cruiser, the best money could buy. It had weapons for defense, of course, but its primary function was to house Ambassador Aralias as he made his way from galaxy to galaxy on his missions. Some of those missions were sanctioned and made public, although most of them had been top secret and funded by the Denards. In fact, the Ambassador's crew was made up exclusively of Denards, all of them hiding in plain sight while donning the UGFS official uniforms.

The crew was loyal to a fault to my husband. And although they respected me as his wife, obeyed my commands as long as their beloved leader wasn't around, and said order didn't conflict with any of his, they all had looked the other way when it'd come to the abuse Amir had inflicted upon me. Granted, some of the younger crew members couldn't make eye contact with me, but none of them had ever lifted a finger to help me. Not once.

My hand trembled as I punched in the code to my old room. The ghost of my torment lingered, memories from what seemed like a lifetime ago causing my heart to thrash, and my breath to come out in short spurts. I half expected Amir to stride around the corner, to take me by my hair, and to commence with a beating right there in the hallway.

No. Stop. He's dead. He can't hurt you anymore. And even if he was still alive, you're different. You would fight back this time.

Notching my chin up, I entered my room, heaving a sigh of relief when the door slid shut behind me. I'd told Silver that I needed a few minutes before talking to anyone after what had happened. I'd also informed him that I wanted to speak to my father, or at least my mother as soon as contact could be made.

"Ressi," I whispered, tapping on my wristband. "Where are you? I need to talk to you." She didn't respond. Flipping open the band, I peered at the small screen, which was suspiciously blank. Snorting, I snapped it shut. She was definitely up to something, and I wondered if she even knew what was going on and where I was.

Unbidden, an image of Amir and me flashed in my mind.

He stood over me while I cowered in bed, having been awoken from a fitful slumber. "I called for you, why didn't you respond?"

"I-I was sleeping."

"With who? Who were you sleeping with?" Throwing my blankets off of me, he stormed around my room in search of an imaginary lover. It was a twisted game of his, to accuse me of seducing members of his crew, as if he was jealous. I knew better. He wasn't jealous in the traditional sense. He simply viewed me as his, and even though he didn't want me, he certainly wouldn't stand for anyone else touching what belonged to him.

"Amir, please. There's no one here but me."

"Then why didn't you answer my call?" He flung one of my discarded shoes at me, the hard bottom slamming into my forearm as I blocked my face.

Shaking my head, I dislodged the memory, forcing it back where it belonged—in the deep, dark place that I never visited, the one I hoped to close for good.

Reaching for the table beside me without looking, I grabbed the first object my fingers found, a book maybe, and I hurled it across the room, the sound it made as it smashed into a mirror satisfying. Very satisfying indeed.

Blindly, rage guiding me, I picked up another object and threw it as hard as I could across the room. And then another. And another. The tinkling of glass, the foul aroma of perfumes mixing, and the snapping of wood, were all music to my ears, a symphony of purging. A rhythm of eradicating my past.

Never again. Never again. Never again.

A few minutes later, or hours, my sense of time skewed, I dropped to my knees, chest heaving, and my skin slick with sweat. Surveying the damage to my once pristine room, my mouth tugged up at the corners, my fangs catching on my lower lip. I knew they were just things, objects that held no significance to me, or to my dead husband, but … but they'd been a part of my life with him, and I wanted to erase them, even if it was merely a symbolic gesture.

He's dead. Jane killed him. And yet … The memory of the last time I'd seen him remained fresh, just like all the others.

"I will make you pay for this, Nina," Amir snarled, his knuckles going white around the metal bars of his prison cell.

Notching my chin up, I narrowed my eyes. "You've made me pay quite enough over the years." My hand unerringly found and traced along one of the larger scars on my face. "And to think I ever thought I loved you."

"You're a traitor to the Denards, your own kind. Your father won't deny me your death when he hears of this."

Rage suffused my system, causing me to vibrate with it. "Then it's a good thing no one outside of this ship will ever hear anything from you again."

He laughed, the sound causing chills to race up my spine. "It's him, isn't it? That hu-mutt you tainted yourself with before we were married? I know he was on this ship. I know you saw him." He stood, his face contorted into a mask of hatred. "I won't just kill you. I'll make you watch me torture and kill him first.

I'll pick him apart piece by piece. And he'll die knowing it was all because of you."

I stared at him, my husband, the man who had tormented me all of these years. Cold indifference washed over me. I feel nothing. Absolutely nothing. I hope Jane makes it painful for him. *Pivoting on my heels, I left the room.*

The chime on my door sounded. Pulling myself to my feet, I shuffled over to enter in the unlock code, pausing to run my hands over my face to check for any wolfy changes. *Phew. Back to normal.* When the door slid open, Silver stood on the other side, his expression pinched with worry.

"I heard some noise in here …" His eyes widened as he peeked around me to see the disaster I'd left in my wake. "What happened?"

I smiled. "Just doing some rearranging. Nothing for you to worry about." Moving past him, I stepped into the hall. "Thin walls on this ship. Sorry if the racket I made disturbed anyone. I usually try to be quiet." My words were laced with double meaning, and by the flush in his cheeks, I knew he was aware of it. *Yeah, that's right. Butt into my business when I smash up a few knick-knacks, but when my husband beat me, pretend like nothing's wrong.*

Humanity, something the Denards were terrified of losing … but what was it really? I mean, I knew what it was by definition, but I'd never experienced it myself. I'd witnessed more compassion from other species, incapable of humanity by its very definition, than I'd ever felt from my people. Did the Denards become something else besides human? Had they forgotten what it was like to be human simply because they no longer went by the name? Was I somehow more in touch with my humanity now that I was genetically less of one?

Silver cleared his throat. "Right. Well, we contacted your parents and they requested a meeting ... in person. They are also quite concerned with the state of things."

"No word from Amir—I mean Ambassador Aralias yet?"

"No. Not a peep. And no one seems to have a clue as to where he is. This isn't like him, which is why the crew is worried."

"Who's the last person to have seen him?"

"Not sure, maybe Johnny. At least that's what he thought. He was hoping you'd had contact though."

I nodded. *Good.* I was almost positive no one had known I'd been the last one to see Amir before he'd disappeared, but I wanted to be sure. If someone had, it would have been necessary to concoct a plausible story. "I'm sure he'll turn up soon." At least pieces of him. After all, Jane had jettisoned his ashes out into space. A perverse side of me wanted to laugh, but I managed to hold it in check, remaining stoic on the outside.

"When do my parents arrive?"

"We're going to them."

My claws dug into my palms, the metallic scent of blood accosting my nose. *Keep it calm. This is what you wanted. They're simply making it easier for you.* "Oh? Did they say why?"

Silver shook his head. "No, and I didn't ask."

I snorted. I knew how intimidating my father could be. My mother was always at his side, but she rarely said much, her presence more for show of solidarity than anything else. "When will we arrive?" I didn't bother asking where, because my parents didn't have a permanent home. Just like most Denards, they roamed the galaxies on their luxurious ships, stopping for short periods of time on colony planets, not wanting to settle down for fear of being discovered and attacked. They led lives of paranoia and hate, blaming the rest of the Universe for their constant state of upheaval, never taking the responsibility for their own choices.

"Well," I leaned against the wall just outside my room, "let me know when we're close so I can make myself presentable."

Silver's eyes darted to my scars and then moved quickly away. The small action said volumes, and it took everything in me not to rip him apart with my bare hands. He thought the scars on my face made it impossible for me to truly be presentable. I was a ruined beauty by his standards. *Funny how when I'm not here amongst my supposed people, I'd almost forgotten about them.*

I sidestepped into my room without another word, sliding the door shut in Silver's face. "I'll show you not presentable," I growled, scraping my claws down the wall.

Chapter 22

Hunched over a long shard of glass, I stared at myself with cold indifference. I'd showered, and dressed, discarding my soiled clothes for a crisp, grey, one-piece pants combo. It was what I'd normally wear when in Amir's presence, him preferring me to do my best to blend into the background. I had to present myself as the same browbeaten wife as the crew had come to know, but I was no longer her. I'd buried that woman the moment I'd decided to hand Amir over to Jane.

Tracing the scars along my cheeks, I considered them. For so long I'd hated the blemished flesh, been ashamed. But now the pattern of misshapen skin represented all I'd gone through on my journey to become who I was today. And I was beginning to like the new me. She was stronger and more self-assured. She had the fortitude to face her past, even when she didn't have to because it's what needed to be done despite the pain and turmoil it caused her. It was possible that I could learn to love myself just the way I was, my scars a badge of honor for the warrior I'd become.

I chuckled, the sound humorless. *Warrior? I'm not a warrior.* The only one I'd ever fought against was myself. Of course, since you can't escape the hateful words in your head, sometimes a war within yourself is the most difficult to win.

"Oh, whatever." Unfurling myself to my full height, I kicked the glass with my boot. I didn't have time for existential analysis of any kind. I had to fortify myself mentally for the meeting with my parents. I needed to get as much information from them as possible about what the Denards were up to, and the only way I could do that was by pretending to be as clueless and weak as I used to be.

"Angst, angst, angst!" Ressi hissed, clutching her head. "I swear, I thought it would get better after you got it on with Maddox, but here you are, still overthinking and over—just being over the top about everything just like usual."

"Where've you been? I could have used you a few times over the last couple of hours." Her outfit had changed, again, an eerie facsimile of Jane's latest Steampunk ensemble adorning her tiny, furry body. "Please tell me you weren't off coding new clothes. Please tell me my A.I. isn't that frivolous."

She sniffed, running a paw over her whiskers. "No, of course not. I was attempting to take over Xorik's ship. But that didn't really work out." Her tail swished back and forth. "So then to make myself feel better I coded myself a few new outfits."

"Of course you did."

She threw her hands up in the air. "But I'm here now."

I rolled my eyes. "So I'm the dramatic one, huh?"

Her nose twitched. "Yes. It's you. Definitely not me."

Laughing, I swatted at her, and she swam through the air out of my reach. Ressi was the comic relief I needed in my life. She was right about me taking things too seriously sometimes. It was nice to have someone ridiculous to pull me out of it, and to remind me that none of us get out of life alive. "I'm sure you already know, but I'm going to be meeting with my parents soon."

She nodded, landing on the edge of a broken chair. She scanned my handiwork. "I like what you did with the place. It's very Lunin chic."

Quirking an eyebrow, I deadpanned, "Lunin chic?"

"Yes. Rowr." She extended her claws, running them through the air. "It's one way to shake things up."

"Mmm," I grunted, "I suppose."

My door chimed. Glancing down the line of my body, I ran my hands along the crisp material of my top and pants. My heart thudded lazily, at peace with what was to come even though the rest of me was on edge. Or maybe Maddox and Kade were right and the beast inside of me was a separate entity, and she was calm when I was not.

Either way, the underlying tranquility was reassuring, causing the rest of me to fall in line.

Inhaling sharply, I strode for the door, ready for whatever hand would be dealt me.

"WHAT PLANET IS THIS?" A subdued red glow encased the small globe, casting eerie shadows through the window in our transport.

Silver glanced over his shoulder at me. "Not sure. We were only sent the coordinates."

"We still in the Milky Way?"

"No. We crossed over into— What the hell?" The transport rattled, shifting to the right and then back again. "Tom," Silver said, his voice going up a few octaves, "what's going on?"

Tom, the older, balding pilot, stared at the controls, his expression a mask of confusion. "It's as if someone else is controlling the flight path, but from inside." His gaze went wild, darting around to land on me, the only other person in the transport with us.

I raised my hands. "Don't look at me." When he turned back around, I tapped my wristband, hissing under my breath, "Stop whatever you're doing right now, Ressi. This isn't funny."

Her image flashed in front of me, her tiny body twisting in a victory dance. She then spun around to stick her tongue out at Silver and Tom, before disappearing.

A second later, Tom heaved an audible sigh of relief. "It's fine now. Must have been some kind of mechanical glitch. I'll have it taken in for diagnostics once we've landed."

"Yeah, just a glitch," I muttered. There was no end to the trouble Ressi could cause if she started being able to control ships. We were going to have to have a long talk later. Her antics were crossing over into dangerous territory.

"It shouldn't be much longer," Tom offered. "Five to ten minutes before we touch down."

I nodded, my gaze finding the small planet again. *My parents are somewhere down there.* It had been years since I'd seen them. Not since my marriage to Amir. I'd wondered more times than I could count why they never sent for me, never came to visit. It was as if they'd passed me along to Amir as a possession of sorts, a tool for him, and I'd ceased mattering to them.

What will they say when they see the condition of my face? Will they be angry at Amir, or will my mother make excuses for him like she always did for my father? Or will they blame me for everything?

Bile burned my esophagus, my nails digging into the armrest of my seat. Focusing on my hands, I willed them to stay normal, claws an unwanted side effect of my sudden nerves.

The transport rattled as it passed through the atmosphere, thrusters engaging.

You can do this, and before you know it, you'll be back in Maddox's arms.

Chapter 23

As soon as the transport landed, the doors were forced open from the outside, and several guards, none of who I recognized, stormed aboard.

"Hands up," a short, stalky guard demanded, brandishing a laser pistol.

"Me?" I squeaked. I hadn't been expecting a parade, but being greeted by gunpoint was a bit of a surprise.

"Yes, Nina Aralias, you are being detained for questioning."

Okay. Stay calm. They don't know anything. "For what? You can't do this to me. Do you have any idea who I am?" My gaze flicked down to his UGFS uniform, where the insignia was supposed to be. There was none. "You weren't sent by my parents." Behind my back, my claws lengthened. "Who the hell are you?"

Raising the pistol, the guard squeezed the trigger

twice, hitting Silver and Tom, both of them slumping forward. My eyes widened. *Okay. This is not good. Yeah, thanks, Ms. Captain Obvious.*

Ressi appeared in front of the guards, bobbing and weaving in the air. "Hey! Hey, over here! Bet you can't hit me!"

"What the hell is that thing?" the tall guard by the door yelled.

"Calm down, it's just an A.I. image," the guard beside him snapped. "It's just—"

Taking the opportunity of the distraction offered by Ressi, I bent down and rushed the short guard in front, my shoulder connecting with his soft stomach. With a grunt, he lost his balance, grabbing onto my hair and yanking for support. A snarl ripped from my throat, claws raking across his arms on instinct. He screamed, toppling to the ground in a heap, blood spurting from his bone-deep wounds.

"What the fuck?" one of the other guards exclaimed, backing away. "She's supposed to be a Denard like us." He waved his gun at me, his face paling.

"Don't shoot her. Don't fucking shoot her. She's not worth anything to us dead."

"Who the hell are you and why are you here?" I growled, my fangs slurring my words.

The tall guard squeezed off a few shots, his aim either horrible or he was merely attempting to scare me. It had the opposite effect. Rage sizzled through my veins, adrenaline surging. With a roar, I leapt, slashing at both of them, my claws tearing through soft flesh and muscle. The scent of fresh blood bloomed in the air, the coppery tang of it filling my nose and sliding over my tongue.

Crouching over the taller of the two guards, I dug the tips of my claws into his neck, careful not to injure him further … yet. "What the hell do you want from me?"

"You're not Nina Aralias, are you?"

"Of course I am." I glanced over at the other guard, his eyes wide and fixated on the ceiling. *Dead.* The third guard, the one who'd seemed in charge, or at least the most ballsy, was splayed out on the floor, bleeding out. His heart thudded weakly.

"No. Nina Aralias is a Denard." He coughed, the sound wet within his lungs. "You're a monster."

Tightening my grip a bit, my claws slid deeper into his flesh. "I'm going to ask one more time … What are you doing here?"

"We thought we could use you as leverage … leverage against your parents."

"But you're Denards, too. Aren't you?" Leaning into him, I sniffed. He smelled human to me, but what the hell did I know? I was new to the whole scent identifier thing. Some things came more naturally to me as a Lunin than others. My sense of smell had been heightened exponentially, but that didn't mean I knew what I was scenting when I got a whiff of it.

"Of course we're Denards." His eyes slid shut, another wet cough wracking his body.

"This one back here is dead," Ressi said.

Standing, I stared down at the guard beneath me. "This one will be too in a few minutes. So much for getting information out of him." I wiped my hands on my pants, the gore smearing across the grey material, turning it crimson. "We need to get out of here and find my parents. I have no idea what's going on."

Ressi floated in front of me, her whiskers vibrating. "Could the reason the Denards haven't made a move after the attacks be because they're fighting internally? It wouldn't be the first time."

I swept my gaze over the five dead bodies, nibbling my bottom lip. "It's possible. With Amir no longer in the picture, there could be a question of leadership. You know my parents placed him in power, someone could want the same for themselves."

"And they'd planned on using you as a pawn to get your parents to do what they want. Makes sense."

Stepping out of the transport, I sucked in a breath of fresh air. "Which means it's probably the case, Occam's razor and all of that."

Ressi bobbled in the air. "I scanned the transport for some kind of map, and this is all I could come up with." A tiny image shimmered into existence directly in front of me. It looked like a toddler had drawn it, complete with X marks the spot.

"What the hell is that supposed to be?" I tilted my head back and forth, attempting to make sense of it.

"There is a set of coordinates above this little blob thing." She pointed at what appeared to be an ink stain.

"I guess it's better than nothing." Raising my hand over my eyes, I peered up at the sky. The red glow I'd seen around the planet from space wasn't as bright on the ground. "Can you get some readings on this place? I want to know what to expect since I'll be going on foot."

"Way ahead of you." Ressi swirled around my head. "The solar system this planet is in has three suns, but it's only close to one of them. I won't bore you with all the science stuff since I can already see your eyes glazing over … let's just say it's going to be hot as hell during the day."

My forehead crinkled in confusion. "Umm … doesn't seem that bad to me." Sure, I was sweating, but I wasn't terribly uncomfortable. I'd classify the planet as not pleasant, but not unpleasant either. "Maybe your readings are off. Check again."

Ressi scrunched up her face at me. "I don't need to check again. It's not hot now because it's the middle of the night."

My eyebrows lifted in shock. "What?" I took in our surroundings … sand, sand, sand, oh, and more sand. *Shit.* "Why would my parents settle on a desert planet, even if it is temporary?"

Ressi shrugged. "Guess you can ask them, if you live that long."

I scowled. "Now is not the time to ditch your optimism."

"I find being a realist is much more efficient."

Of course she did. But wait. Snapping my fingers, I grinned. "What about those men? They had to have some kind of transportation to get here. They certainly didn't walk and they don't live out here in the open desert. We can take their ride."

"It'll probably be easier to ditch the dead bodies and take the transport," Ressi said. "Because those men did a really good job of hiding their ship. It's not showing up with any scans."

I scrubbed a hand down my face, the lingering scent of blood assaulting my nose, the odor clinging to my skin. I snorted in an attempt to expel the aroma. *Shit.* I had absolutely no desire to haul those dead bodies out of the transport. Even with their decomposing corpses no longer inside, the stench of blood and decay would be overwhelming for a Lunin like me. I wasn't sure I could handle it. But then again … if it was a choice between my survival and death …

"Guess I'm hauling those bodies out of the transport."

"Wise choice," Ressi said.

"Hmm … well, you know me, my new life is all about making the smart choices."

"Nina! Neens, talk to me! I need to hear your voice! Are you okay?"

Staggering, I clutched my head, pain shooting through it as Maddox's voice ricocheted around my skull. "Maddox, please, don't shout like that. It might liquefy my brain."

"Oh, thank God. I got a flash of some men pulling guns on you."

"I'm fine. Them, not so much."

"See, she's fine. I told you," Xorik's sardonic tone wafted through my mind.

"Hey. How are you both talking to me at the same time? My head is not a group chat of some sort."

"Your mate was having trouble connecting with you, so I offered to open the path. Over time, he should be able to do it himself."

"Neens, fuck. I was—I was terrified. I thought I was going to lose you."

"No worries. I promised I'd come back to you, and I will."

"I wish I was there with you to keep you safe."

I snorted and rolled my eyes. "I did fine on my own. But I wouldn't mind your help hefting some dead bodies right about now."

"I love you, Neens. Do you hear me? I love you and you come—"

It went silent in my mind. Growling under my breath, I cursed out Xorik. I had the impression that he'd cut off the mind link because he didn't want to deal with hearing Maddox and I profess our love for each other. *Bitter asshole.*

Ressi danced in front of me, her face pinched with worry. "You better get a move on. It'll be daylight soon."

Fuck. It was time to get to work.

Chapter 24

Sweat leaked from every pore in my body, and my tongue felt like sandpaper in my mouth. I shoved at some blonde hair that had escaped from my braid, the strands sticking to my face and neck. But I paused for only a moment, knowing if I stopped now it could mean death by sunstroke. Daylight had broken only minutes ago, and yet the heat was stifling on a level I'd never experienced before. Ressi had been right about me not living to talk to my parents if I'd attempted to walk across this planet during the day, and even the choice of waiting it out in the shade of the transport probably wouldn't have done the job with no water to relieve my desperate thirst.

"Just one more to go," I mumbled, swallowing thickly. "One more and we can be on our way." I was almost tempted to leave the last body where it was, but I knew it'd be a mistake in the long run.

Lurching onto the transport, I held the breath in my lungs. Bending down to grab a hold of the last dead guard's body, I grimaced. Small black bugs wiggled within the torn flesh, reminding me of maggots, although they definitely weren't. These things had wings and tiny sharp pinchers, which they were using to tear at the rotting flesh. *Ew! Ew! Ew!*

I dragged the guard out into the blinding light, squinting, spots dancing in front of my eyes despite my efforts. His bloated head thunked on each of the three steps on the way out, leaving a pale slime behind. I'd seen a lot of dead bodies in my life, courtesy of my dearly departed husband, but I'd never witnessed slime of any kind oozing out of them. It was a wonderful side effect of being on a foreign planet where everything was unknown to me. Even Ressi couldn't find answers in her database.

"Oh, look, it turns green when it oxidizes," she exclaimed, her face hovering precariously close to the sludge.

"Mmm … great that you find it so interesting, especially because you're an A.I. and can't smell any of it. I'm lucky I haven't been overcome by the noxious fumes of these rotting corpses."

Dropping the guard near the other four bodies, I swiped at my brow with the back of my arm. A wave of dizziness assaulted me, and I plodded back towards the transport, each step bogged down with exhaustion. Once inside, I flopped into the flight chair, blinking the controls into focus.

"Okay, Ressi, what were those coordinates?" I yawned, sleep tugging at me. My eyes fluttered as my head swam. "You know what? I need just a little nap. Like five minutes —five minutes and I'll be okay." Slumping over onto my arm, I closed my eyes, another yawn wracking my body. "Just five minutes ..."

"Come here," Maddox commanded, his chocolate eyes sparking with gold. "I don't understand why you're so far away."

Splayed out across my small bed on The Pittsburgh, Maddox was completely naked, not a stitch of clothing on his sculpted body. I allowed my gaze to travel over him, blatantly ogling. His olive skin glowed in the dim lighting, the rise and fall of his chest highlighting the ripples of muscle. He was lithe, toned from training with the New Earth military, the years of it having changed his form to solid perfection.

I prowled closer, licking my lips as I thought of tracing his six-pack with my tongue before going lower.

"What are you thinking?" he purred, drawing a hand down his stomach.

"About how I wished we hadn't been separated all those years."

Sitting up, he ran a hand through his hair. "Let's not talk about that. I want to concentrate on the now."

"You still never told me your number."

His gaze darkened, a scowl twisting his full lips. "Yeah, I don't want to talk about that either."

"Mmm ..." I slid my palms over his knees, dropping down onto mine. Dancing my fingers along his inner thighs, I stared

up the line of his body, smiling when his cock jumped with excitement. "What do you want to talk about then?"

"Talking is overrated."

"Sometimes." I pressed several kisses along his leg, drawing closer to where he wanted me.

"The numbers don't matter, Neens, so if your plan is to tease the answer out of me, think again."

I huffed. That's exactly what I'd been planning on doing. Sitting back on my haunches, I glared at him. "I just ... I just feel like we're not connecting." I shook my head. "No, that's not right. I feel like there's a wall or space between us. We're not settled, Maddox."

He regarded me with bewilderment. "I've told you I love you, we've had sex half a dozen times since I woke up ... oh, and we're mated. How much closer can we get?"

All those things were true, and yet there was still something missing. I couldn't quite put my finger on it. "There's some kind of disconnect," I tapped my temple, "up here. I'm not sure what it is." Although I had a general idea. I'd watched all the couples on The Pittsburgh, witnessed how each of them had become a team ... I didn't feel that way with Maddox.

He leaned forward, cradling my chin. "What can I do to make you feel better about us? And it's not just the number thing. Don't you trust me? Is that what it is? Do you think I'm going to walk away from you again?"

Tears pooled in the corners of my eyes. "Maybe. I don't know." My hands curled into fists, and I tapped my knuckles against the ground. "I wish I knew. It's just something isn't right between us."

"Come on, Neens, talk to me. You can tell me anything."

"Can I? Can I tell you absolutely anything?"

Hurt swam across his visage, tightening the muscles in his jaw. "Of course you can."

"I guess ... I don't know. We met when we were so young, and even though we loved each other we never got to know each other. How much do we really know about each other and our lives? What if there are things that one of us can't accept from our pasts?"

"You're afraid to get comfortable, truly comfortable because you think you're unlovable. You think there are things that will turn me away from you."

I nodded, a lump forming in my throat. "I could have left him. Why didn't I? Why did I stay?" A guttural sob tore from my chest. "I thought ... once, I thought I loved him. How could I have been such a fool? I let him trap me, and I stayed. I stayed all those years." Crumpling in on myself, I wrapped my arms around my middle.

"No, oh God, Neens, no." Scooping me up in his arms, he settled on the bed with me, his hot breath cascading over my hair. "What can I do? Tell me ..."

Pressing my face into his chest, I sniffled. "Talk. I want to talk to you."

"About what?"

"Everything. I want us to talk about everything. I don't want there to be any secrets between us. And then after all of that, if you tell me you still love me and won't walk away, then I'll believe you."

His fingers dug into my flesh as his arms tightened around me. "If that's what you need, we'll talk ... about everything."

I smiled through my tears. Yes, it's what I wanted ... to talk. To bond beyond the physical, not that I was complaining about our sexual escapades, it was just ... I needed more from him, from me ... for us.

"Nina. Neens, you have to wake up. You have to wake up and drink this for me."

I slitted my eyes open, a fuzzy image of Maddox wavering in front of me. Inhaling, I picked up on his spicy scent, although it was intermingled with blood, death, and decay.

"I'm so glad we talked." My tongue was thick and heavy in my mouth, the effort to move it taxing. "So glad. Now I don't have to worry about you judging me for killing those men."

"Drink this, please." Something solid was pressed to my lips.

I turned my head away. "I don't have to worry about any of it anymore, because I know that you love me. All of me."

My nose pinched together, someone holding my nostrils and forcing my head back. Sputtering to breathe, my mouth swung open. The instant it did, cool liquid poured down my throat. I attempted to swallow it, grateful for the relief, but most of it ran down my chin. After a few moments, I slapped at the hands holding me, wanting to be left alone.

"I'm tired. Just let me sleep."

Ice ran along my forehead, and then the back of my neck. I moaned in pleasure.

"Come on, Neens. Drink a little more. For me. Please, just a little more, and then I can get you out of here."

"Leave me alone," I groaned.

"I will. I promise. Just drink a little more."

Grunting, I accepted the liquid as it coursed down my throat. "There, happy? Now leave me alone."

I was jostled, the sensation of floating overwhelming me. "Mmm … love you, Maddox. So glad we talked."

I slipped back into oblivion.

"SHE'LL BE FINE NOW," Tamzea said. "Heat exhaustion and sunstroke are easy fixes for healers like us."

"Then why isn't she awake yet?" Maddox demanded. "Check again. Check her goddamned vitals again."

"I'm awake," I croaked. "At least for the moment." I attempted to open my eyes, but it was as if they were glued shut. "Just— I want to sleep."

"We healed her. But that doesn't mean her body doesn't need some rest. You need to let her."

There was some rustling, and then warmth suffused my side. Maddox's familiar scent surrounded me, wrapping me in comfort. *I'm safe now.* Sighing, I yawned, slipping back into a deep slumber.

Chapter 25

A strong heartbeat thrummed steadily under my ear, and sweat pooled under my cheek. Opening my eyes, the expanse of Maddox's muscular chest took up my view. My fingers found their way into the spattering of chest hair, twirling languidly.

"Neens," he rumbled. "How are you feeling?"

"Good." I attempted to remember how exactly I'd gotten there, but my mind was only able to pull up fuzzy images. "I think. The last thing I remember is being on that damn red planet, also known as hell, and then …" Had I gone to sleep? Passed out? There was a giant hole where the information should have been.

"You passed out from heat stroke. I sensed something was wrong, and then Ressi contacted us with your coordinates."

"How'd you get past the UGFS cruiser, and what about—"

He pressed a finger to my lips, silencing me. "The Pittsburgh got close with its cloaking device, and I was able to get down to you easily after that."

"I still don't understand who those men were or what happened. They—"

"There are only a handful of lifeforms on that planet. All human. We were waiting for you to wake up to see if you knew anything that Ressi didn't, however unlikely since she was there with you."

My gut churned. "I don't understand any of it. Amir's crew made it seem like the planet was a stronghold, and I was on my way to meet my parents. Usually, the Denard counsel travels with an entourage, and a handful of people is definitely not that."

He tipped my chin up, snagging my gaze with his. "You kept saying you were glad we talked."

"Huh? When?"

"When I came for you. You were delirious for sure, and definitely more than a bit out of it, but you kept saying it over and over again. What did you mean?"

My throat tightened, and my heart took off at a gallop. "It's just … I dreamt about our conversation, you know, the one right before I left?" The tips of my ears heated. "I guess it meant more to me than I realized. Us talking about things, getting to know each other. It made me feel closer to you than I ever did before."

He chuckled. "Women."

I poked his chest. "Hey. You take that back. Or didn't it

mean anything to you?" My chest constricted at the thought. What if all the things we'd shared were only important to me? What if I was reading too much into things and nothing had changed at all?

His warm lips pressed against my forehead. "I guess I didn't realize it before that night, but you were right. We did need to talk. There were a lot of things we needed to sort through. Apparently fucking doesn't fix everything. Who would have thought?" Grinning, he flipped me over, caging me in with his big body. His gaze ran along my face before settling on my eyes. "It meant the world to me, Neens. Don't think because I'm a man that I don't have my doubts too sometimes."

I ran my fingers along his beard. "And now?"

"I have no more doubts. As long as there's breath in both of our bodies, we'll find a way to be together."

His lips slammed into mine, and his pelvis ground against my heated core. A peace settled over me, one driven by more than the mere physical. Even though Maddox and I had been young—so young, when we'd first met, and from completely different worlds, somehow we'd found our way back to each other. Our love had proven to be the real deal, despite the complications.

"No more talking right now, okay? I think we're good on that front for a while," I murmured into his mouth.

His response was to deepen our kiss.

Moaning, I let myself get lost in all things Maddox.

"IS it safe to go anywhere on this ship anymore?" Jane whined. "I mean, seriously … everywhere I turn—"

"Yeah, yeah," I mumbled, a smile playing across my lips. "Everywhere you turn you're getting an eyeful of someone's naked ass." Sitting up, I yanked the blanket over me. "That's what happens when you have a ship full of mated pairs. Besides, Maddox and I won't be here forever. So I need to make sure you look your fill before I'm gone."

"Next time I see your pale ass hanging out on my ship I'm going to shoot it," she growled.

Maddox shifted, tucking me into his side. "You'll do no such thing, Jane."

"Try me."

"She's just cranky because she's bored," Ash offered. "Apparently even I can't keep her completely entertained."

"Not unless you let me target practice on you," she snapped. "I'm just getting antsy because I don't know what the hell is going on."

Sitting up, I scanned the infirmary for my clothes. "Speaking of not knowing what's going on … I need to go back down to that planet to figure out what's happening with the Denards. Something is off about the entire situation."

Maddox ran his hand down my back, eliciting a shiver. "Agreed. But this time I'm going with you."

Sighing, I opened my mouth to protest but snapped it shut again. Was it such a horrible thing that he wanted to protect me? After all, I wanted to do the same for him. If we were going to be a team, then I'd have to make compromises, just as long as he did, too.

"Fine. You can come. But you have to let me take the lead."

"Not a problem."

"Yeah, that's what he says now, but trust me, he's going to try to take control of things anyways. Ash does it all the time." Jane punched Ash in the arm, who smirked at her.

Maddox kissed my temple, his eyes dancing with mirth. "I won't. I promise."

"Promises are made to be broken, isn't that right, Ash?" Jane said.

Maddox bared his teeth at Jane. "Stop trying to cause trouble between me and my mate or maybe I'll shoot *you* in the arm this time."

Flames erupted in her irises. "You wouldn't dare. I'd burn you to a crisp."

Ash heaved an exasperated sigh. "All right. Everyone is tense. We need to concentrate on things besides making idle threats of harm against each other."

"I'm going to get dressed and then we'll head back down to the planet," I announced. "Oh, what happened to Xorik?" I was still suspicious about Maddox being poisoned. I would only trust Xorik tentatively. He needed to prove his loyalty, and even then … I snorted. He didn't matter at the moment. I simply wanted to make sure he wasn't lurking around waiting to cause trouble.

Jane slid the top hat off her head and tapped it against

the wall. "He's in one of the cells below." She sniffed. "Safest place for him."

My lips twitched. Of course she locked him up. Why did I expect any differently? I nudged Maddox with my elbow. "Did he get a chance to talk to you about the mate situation?"

"Yeah, a bit. I said I'd think about introducing him to some people on New Earth that could actually make some kind of deal with him." He shrugged. "I made no promises though."

"Alrighty then." Holding the blanket in front of me, I slid from the cot. Maddox, unabashed, stood without shielding himself.

"Arrrgh!" Jane exclaimed. "Come find us when you're both dressed." She disappeared in a puff of smoke, Ash doing the same a second later.

Maddox wrapped his arms around my middle, pressing into my back. "Think we have time for a quickie?"

My middle warmed. "Depends, is it actually going to be a quickie? Because you know, I don't want to be exactly what Jane accuses us of." He peppered kisses along my bare shoulders, a shiver moving up my spine. "You know, having sex all over the ship instead of doing other more important tasks."

"How am I supposed to find the motivation to do anything except find my way inside of you when you're naked?"

I dropped the sheet when he bent me over the cot,

pushing into me from behind. Reaching forward, my claws tore at the rough material in front of me, shredding it with ease.

Hot lips slid up my spine as he moved slowly within me. I bucked, wanting it harder ... rougher.

"Fuck me like you mean it, Maddox."

Straightening up, he snarled, ramping up his pace. His claws dug into my hips, holding me firm, and I arched back to meet him with every thrust.

"Yes, yes, fuck yes!"

A kaleidoscope of colors exploded behind my closed lids, my toes and fingers curling tightly as I fell over the edge, my body freefalling into ecstasy.

"Fuck, Neens. So good—fuuuuck."

Building a brutal pace, Maddox forced several more orgasms on my body, the bliss of them staggering. He fell over my back, pumping an irregular rhythm as he pulsed his release into me, words of adoration spilling from his lips.

His tongue snaked out to lick the sweat off the back of my neck. "Think we need a shower now. Probably should take it together. You know, because the water is limited even with the Gartian filtration system. Wouldn't want Jane to come gunning for us because she couldn't get a shower with real water."

Glancing over my shoulder, I delivered him a faux scowl. "You wouldn't be trying to sneak in another quickie in the shower, would you?"

One side of his mouth quirked up. "Me? Never."

"Mmm hmmm."

Chapter 26

I didn't think I'd ever been so clean in my entire life. Maddox had made sure to wash every nook and cranny on my entire body, most of them with his tongue first.

"You're making me feel like a piece of meat," Maddox said. He dropped his towel a moment later, and wiggled his perfectly sculpted ass, grinning.

I sniggered. "Yes, you seem so put out by it. Why don't you dance around naked some more to show me just how much you hate me ogling you."

"You would just love that, wouldn't you?" He pressed his index fingers over his nipples. "I have thoughts and feelings, too. You can't just use me for sex."

Snorting, I slipped a black T-shirt over my head. Maddox was acting so carefree and ... silly. It made my insides sing that he felt that comfortable around me now. I'd seen glimpses of the humorous side of him years ago, but not since we'd been reunited, or not until now. It made me feel connected, and content, like he wasn't afraid to be his true self around me.

Warmth bloomed in my middle, and my chest constricted, a lump forming in my throat. *I love him so goddamn much. I never thought it would be possible to love someone so much.*

Fully clothed, I glided past him to the door. "All right, Mr. Sensitive, hurry up and get some clothes on so we can head back down to find my parents. I'm sure Jane isn't going to be pleased about us taking so long to get ready."

"Not my fault you're insatiable."

"Yeah, *I'm* the one who's insatiable." Chuckling, I made my way out into the corridor, leaving a naked prancing Maddox behind.

Ressi swooped down in front of my face, scowling. "It's about time. I thought you two would never come up for air."

I swatted at her. "I'm sure you kept yourself busy."

"That's not the point. I had stuff I wanted to tell you."

"Yeah, like what?" I made a right at the end of the hallway, stopped, glanced back and forth, and then went left instead. My stomach was demanding a meal, and it would not be denied.

"The lifeforms on the planet are dwindling."

What? That couldn't be right. "How many are left?"

"Three."

Staggering, I leaned against the smooth metal wall. I blinked up at my A.I., my mind reeling. "Have you been able to get a closer look?" What was going on down on that desert planet? Did they not have supplies? Were they dying of dehydration and heatstroke, like I almost had? It just didn't make sense. Silver recently had contact with my parents, and they would have reported a systems failure of any kind. Whatever was going on was a very recent development.

Ressi's ears flattened, and her tail twitched. "No. Something is blocking me from getting closer, which is strange that we're able to get any reading at all if they have a tech shield of any kind up."

I considered skipping food, but my stomach gurgled, letting me know that would be a choice I'd regret. *Shit.* Maddox and I had gotten lost in each other and wasted too much time. I'd rationalized and told myself that nothing in the future is guaranteed, and we have to take the precious moments we had together when we had the chance, but … *No. It wasn't a mistake. Nothing with Maddox ever is. The timing of everything just sucks.*

Shoving off the wall, I sprinted for the eating lounge. It was empty when I got there, and I rummaged through the storage units to find anything that would be halfway edible. Surprisingly, or maybe not so surprisingly, considering Jane and her love of everything related to Earth, I found a tin of oatmeal. It wasn't my favorite, but at least I knew what it was.

A few minutes later, I flopped into a seat at the large table and began shoveling the bland sludge into my mouth. *Sustenance is sustenance, and beggars can't be choosers.*

Jane strode into the room, her gaze falling on the bowl of oatmeal. "I wouldn't recommend eating that. I bought it a while back from someone who told me it was an Earth delicacy." She scrunched up her nose. "It tastes like crap."

"I've had worse," I muttered around a mouthful of the bland food. "The Ambassador made sure I had nothing I could enjoy, and that included what I ate." I carefully kept my mind from conjuring up any memories of my time with Amir, content with letting him stay where he belonged, in the past.

"He was a sick fuck." Flames sprang to life in her irises.

"Yes, he was." I'd often wondered if Amir had always been broken, or if my being with Maddox had caused something to snap in him. *No. None of it was your fault. You hold no blame for Amir's actions.*

Finished with the oatmeal, I shoved the bowl to the side, perching my elbows on the table. "Tell me, Jane. Do you trust me now?"

Mirroring me, she perched her elbows on the table as well. "Weirdly enough, I do." Her lips curled up. "I know all about finding yourself in a situation where you have to do things that aren't ideal to survive." Her expression shuttered as she lost herself in a memory.

"But you kicked me off the ship."

She cleared her throat, her vacant gaze focusing back in on me. "Eh, you know why I kicked you off. I made no secret of it. And clearly it all worked out in the end." She slapped her palms down on the table. "But don't you dare go talking to anyone about it."

I smiled. “No, wouldn’t want anyone to think you cared about such things as love.”

“It would ruin my rep.”

“Mmm hmm.” I was sure the crew on The Pittsburgh were already well aware of Jane’s soft and squishy insides. They just knew better than to let her be privy to that information.

“Look, I know, at least to some degree,” she motioned to the scars on my face, “what you had to go through while you were on that ship with Ambassador Aralias. But I also know that there are things you’ll never share—things I would never understand. None of it matters though, you found your way eventually.”

“But why do you trust me?”

She dropped her gaze to study her nails as she picked at them. “Because I trust my gut. It’s never wrong.”

Ash flamed into the room, placing his hands on her shoulders. “Never? Your gut is never wrong?”

Dropping her head back so she could meet his gaze, she glared at him. “No, never. I did hook up with you on instinct.”

“What about—”

Jane shoved her chair back, the top of it slamming into Ash’s stomach. He doubled over, a smirk on his face. “Really, Jane? You’re so violent.”

She leaned into his face. “You love it, otherwise you wouldn’t pick fights with me all the time.”

His gaze heated. “I do love our foreplay.”

Without breaking eye contact with Ash, Jane said, “You

come find us the minute you're back from the planet." The two of them turned to flame and shot out of the room.

"Hey!" Zula exclaimed. "Watch it! I don't want to be burned alive just because the two of you are in a hurry to get it on and aren't watching where you're going."

"Maybe I wanted to fry your face off," Jane's disembodied voice snarked.

Scooting past Zula, I spared her a tentative smile. "We're heading down to the planet soon to find out what's going on."

Her eyes lit up. "Oh, good. Find me the minute you get back. I'll have questions."

Of course she would. Jogging out into the hallway, I lunged to the left to avoid smacking nose first into Kade's massive chest. "Sorry," I muttered, maneuvering around him.

"No worries."

Smiling to myself, despite the unknown on the red planet, and … well, the unknown about the Denards … I felt good for the first time in as far back as I could remember. And I would fight to hold onto it. Not just for myself, but for the crew on The Pittsburgh as well. In the short period that I'd known them, they'd shown me what it was like to have a real family. Granted, I wasn't a part of it, but they'd allowed me to see that different species could love each other and that they didn't have to be run by hatred like the Denards were. I guess I'd always known it on some level, which was why I'd been open to falling in love with Maddox to begin with, but witnessing it firsthand had changed everything.

Maybe the Denards didn't need to be destroyed. Maybe they just needed to realize the things I already had. Instead of being motivated by revenge … could I let the driving force in me be love and goodwill? For so long I'd been numb, and revenge had given me a reason to push forward, to live, but things had changed yet again … *Yes, I'll fight for love. I'll fight for peace. It's the only way. I see that now. Otherwise, I'm no different than any other Denard, if I let hate be the ultimate motivator.*

Chapter 27

"I don't like this. Something's off." Maddox leaned forward, his nose touching the window of our small pod.

I smacked at his shoulder. "Sit down, and be patient. I thought you were a trained military man, not a five-year-old."

He gave me side-eye, his lips twisting into a frown. "What does me having a bad feeling about something have to do with being a five-year-old? None of what you just said makes sense."

I smacked at him again. "Just sit down, you're making me more nervous than I already am."

Smirking, he dropped into his seat. "You could have just said that to begin with instead of insulting me."

Whatever. I sniffed. "We should be there soon according to the coordinates. Three or four minutes, tops."

My stomach churned as my nerves ratcheted up. We had no idea what we were going to find when we got to the Denard stronghold. Out of the hundreds of lifeforms that should have registered, it was down to three. *Are they all dead, or have they bolted?* But if they bolted, why leave behind three people? Did it have something to do with the men in the faux UGFS uniforms who had attacked me? And what about the cruiser, why weren't they privy to what was going on? In fact, why hadn't they sent anyone down to check on the status of things? Surely they had to know my meeting had gone awry when Silver and Tom hadn't checked in.

Maddox grabbed my hand, squeezing it gently. "We'll have the answers soon enough."

I tilted my head quizzically. "Were you in my head just now?" I kept wondering when our mental connection would strengthen. I wouldn't mind being able to have secret conversations with him. The fact that Xorik trounced into my brain unannounced whenever he felt like it, and yet Maddox couldn't, was beyond annoying.

"No. Or not really. I got sort of an emotional impression. Not actual thoughts."

"Mmm." It was a start.

"But really I wouldn't have even needed that. Your thoughts are written all over your face."

The shuttle shimmied, and the lights brightened, signaling our landing.

"This is it," I muttered. Maddox was right though,

something was off about the entire situation. "I hope this isn't a trap of some sort."

"You and me both," he grumbled.

The engines shut down, the cooling mechanisms humming loudly as they worked overtime in the sweltering environment.

Ressi bobbed around the control panel, nibbling at her paws. "We're inside a hangar, at least the sun won't be beating down on you again." She glanced at me. "There doesn't seem to be anyone around to greet us."

"With only three lifeforms registering, I'm not surprised." Maddox checked his weapons, his hands moving over the holsters deftly. "Ready?"

"As I'll ever be." Heart pounding, I stepped up to the door and hit the unlock code. With a hiss, it slid open, a wave of heat blasting me in the face.

Maddox shoved in front of me. "I'll go first."

I barreled into his side with my shoulder. He grunted in annoyance. "No, I'm going first. You're my backup, not the other way around. You're lucky I let you come at all." Jane was right about him attempting to take over. Well, not this time. As much as I loved Maddox, I wasn't about to let him run the show. Partners took turns, and this mission was my time to be in charge.

"I'll watch the ship. Make sure it stays cool for when you come back," Ressi called from inside. I snorted. The mechanisms that made her go were in my wristband, so technically she'd be with me the entire time, but if she wanted to pretend her 3D image was actually her body, I was done arguing with her. Frankly, I didn't know how she did half the things she did. I wouldn't have been surprised if she told me she was no longer tethered to me and could hop from one machine to another. *Wait. Maybe she can?*

At the door to the main compound, we paused, a smear of crimson catching both of our attention. Leaning in, I sniffed. "Blood."

Maddox nodded. The door was unlocked, and we slid through it cautiously. "Guess we won't be needing these." He tapped his utility belt which held the explosives we'd brought in case we'd need to force an entry somewhere.

"I guess—" The acrid scent of blood, death, and decay punched me in the face. I threw my arm over my nose and mouth, but it was too late. Doubling over, I gagged against my skin, bile shooting up my throat.

Maddox spun me around, quickly attaching a piece of cloth around my face. It didn't completely fix the problem, but it made things more manageable. Straightening, I noted he'd donned a similar mask.

"How'd you know we'd need these?"

"I've been on a few more missions than you since I was spliced with Lunin DNA. My team came to learn that as amazing as our heightened senses can be at times, others they can be a detriment."

"Right."

Resuming our trek down the narrow hallway, he kept silent, listening for signs of life. We'd been directed to go to the center of the compound to find the three remaining lifeforces, but both of us were still convinced there had to be a mistake of some kind, or that we were walking into a trap.

"Shit." Stumbling, I righted myself by nearly faceplanting into a wall.

Glancing down to see what was laying in the middle of the hallway floor, I sucked in a sharp breath. It was a body. Or at least what was left of one. The male Denard was missing his arms and legs, and half of his face. There was no blood, dry or otherwise, anywhere near the body. What was left of the corpse was collapsing in on itself, as if it was rotting away, or something was eating at the flesh.

I crouched down to get a better look and noticed green sludge like I'd seen coming from the bodies I'd moved off the transport. "You see that?" I pointed at the green goo.

Maddox crouched down beside me, his eyes narrowing as he studied the area I was directing his attention to. "What the hell is that? You think it could be from decomposing on this planet? I've seen some strange shit before."

"I don't know. Ressi was quite intrigued when I saw the same thing oozing out of one of the bodies from before. She couldn't find any information about it in any known database though."

"We should get a sample then." Snapping on gloves that he seemingly produced from nowhere, Maddox scooped some of the resin into a tube, capping it tightly, and then sealing it in an airtight tin.

I lifted an eyebrow. "You have a call to get samples from dead bodies often?"

Dropping the tin in his pocket, he snapped off the gloves and tossed them on the ground. "Usually it's soil samples, but yeah, it's happened before. Sometimes a new disease is discovered, and the scientists of New Earth want to make sure that the citizens of New Earth aren't in danger."

Moving around the corner, all further questions were sucked from my brain. "Oh my God," I murmured.

"Fuck," Maddox grunted at the same time.

Half a dozen more bodies lay strewn about, all of them decomposing like the first unlucky bastard we'd come across. Not all of them were missing their limbs, but there was a consistency with the rotting flesh and the green sludge.

"How many Denards did you say usually travel with this colony?"

"Hundreds."

Carefully stepping around the bodies, I tried not to register what some of the squishing sounds were. Even with the mask on, the stench made my eyes water, and bile repeatedly push up my esophagus.

"The three lifeforms should be through this door." I waved my hand in front of me. "I'm guessing it's not locked either."

Pushing into the main part of the compound, my eyes alighted on a familiar face. My mother. Frozen in place, I stared at her prone form. She was slumped against the wall, her green eyes meeting mine with confusion. Her long, blonde hair had fallen out of her head, leaving bloody patches of scalp, and her left hand was missing, along with her right foot.

Suddenly I was in motion, sprinting for her. "Mother!" I dropped down to my knees, my hands fluttering around her. I was afraid to touch her, not sure if I could help or cause her more pain than was already reflected in her gaze.

"Nina," she rasped. "What are you doing here? Now you're going to die, too."

A lump replaced the bile in my throat, and I struggled to find my words. It'd been years since I'd been in contact with my mother, and she and my father were the ones responsible for my marriage to Amir, but—but she was still my mother. No matter what had happened before, how I'd imagined revenge, I didn't want that in my heart. I simply wanted them to love me for who I was. Even if it would never happen now.

"What's going on? I don't understand any of this."

She coughed, the sound wet. "The Galvrarons. They double-crossed us."

I blinked, trying to process her words. "What? You need to explain. I don't know what you're talking about." I resisted the urge to scan the room, knowing that my father was either dead or dying, not wanting the image of his decaying body in my mind forever alongside my mother's.

"We made a bargain for a new kind of airborne, highly

infectious—" She coughed, doubling over as blood sprayed from her mouth. Wiping at her lips with her sleeve, she grimaced, and then continued, "The virus, we planned to release it … everywhere … it was to kill off all of the targeted species. All of them. But instead, it only infected us …"

My eyes widened, the implications of what she was saying finally registering. The Denards had once loosed a virus, later to become known as the G-Pox, that had nearly wiped out the Gartians. Those who had survived replaced their rotting pieces with their special grade of alloy, essentially turning themselves into cyborgs. Were the Denards trying to do it again, but on a much larger scale?

Standing, I clapped a hand in front of my mask. "The attacks were a distraction so you could get the virus out there. They were merely step one in your plan so you could spread the virus to all those planets."

"And we did," she coughed, "but they double-crossed us. The virus wasn't supposed to affect anyone with human DNA."

"But what about the New Earth spliced humans? What about—"

"You mean the hu-mutts? Don't … know …" My mother crumpled in on herself, her eyes glazed over and fixated.

It all clicked into place. I wheeled around, and my gaze snagged Maddox's. "The poison—the poison that nearly killed you. It wasn't a poison at all."

"Fuck. Was I … I could have been infected on Zeffrin, which means—"

"Anyone with human DNA is in danger. We need to get back to The Pittsburgh immediately."

My thoughts swirled as we hurried back to our shuttle. If the virus was so contagious then why hadn't Jane, or me for that matter, been infected? Why had Maddox been the only one to fall ill? And why had Mikla told us that it was a poison? Surely he would have been able to tell the difference between a highly infectious disease, and a synthetic poison. Something there didn't add up.

Who am I kidding? Nothing anywhere is adding up. Mikla had to have known what he was treating Maddox for. After all, his people were the ones who'd double-crossed the Denards.

Panic overtook me the more I considered our dilemma. The Denards had been planning on wiping out … fuck, who knew how many species? All of them from what my mother had said. But the tables had been turned, or so it seemed. Unless …

"What if the virus affects more than anyone with human DNA? What if the Denards have essentially let loose something that will end life from one end of the Universe to the other?"

Maddox grabbed my hand, squeezing it hard. "No. If the Galvrarons had something to do with this then it isn't a mistake. They purposely turned the tables on the Denards. Unfortunately, their species is cold enough to view all of humankind, even New Earth citizens, as worthwhile collateral damage."

A moment later, we arrived at the shuttle. "Ressi, we need to get out of here now," Maddox commanded. "Punch in the coordinates and fire up the engines."

Numbly, I flopped into my seat, buckling myself in. Adrenaline surged through my system, my heart wanting to pound out of my chest. "Come on, Ressi, you heard him. We need to get out of here now."

The engine jumped to life, the shuttle shaking as we launched into the air. Only when we were finally hurtling towards space did the rest hit me.

My parents are dead. Most of the Denards—humans—are dead. I wasn't sure how I truly felt about that. I'd decided I would forgo my need for revenge, wanting to let peace and love be my life motivator. But somehow I'd gotten it anyways, or at least it had been delivered.

Tears spilled from my eyes. If I was being honest with myself, a part of me had hoped to sweep into the Denard stronghold and somehow convince them of the error of their ways. I had hoped to make them all see that hate wasn't the way, that their fears were unbiased, and that all of us could share the Universe because there was room enough for everyone.

Now I'd never get that chance.

I glanced at Maddox, who was staring at me, his golden gaze filled with concern. "You gonna be okay?"

A flash of him lying in the infirmary, unconscious, played across my mind. "I'm not worried about me, at least not much. I'm worried about you. Mikla is going to check you out the minute we step back on the ship."

"He's checking you out, too. You're part human as well."

"I'll let him run some tests on me just to make you happy, but you're going first. And then Jane. You were the only one who was infected before. I want to make sure you don't get sick again. And you're forgetting, I wasn't spliced, so I'm not really human in any way anymore. But you and Jane both are."

Maddox bared his teeth. "You're going first. End of story. We don't even know if what happened to me has anything to do with the virus."

Okay ... denial much? Of course what happened to you had to do with the virus.

Turning my head, I decided to ignore him. I wasn't in the mood to have a silly argument with him. Besides, he would be going first, even if I had to knock him unconscious to make it happen.

Chapter 28

A gnawing, hollow sensation had taken up residence in my gut. Until I knew exactly what we were dealing with, and that Maddox was safe, I wouldn't be able to function properly.

Clambering onto The Pittsburgh, I pushed past Jane and Ash, tugging Maddox straight to the medical wing. Without a word, they trailed along behind us, obviously picking up on my desperation.

Bursting into the infirmary, I found Tamzea and Eron cuddled together on a cot. They both shot up, worry etched into their features when they got a look at me.

Tamzea's hands fluttered around me, assessing. "What's wrong? Who's injured?"

"No one." I shoved Maddox forward. "But he needs to be checked out by you and tested by Mikla. That poison, well, I don't think it was a poison at all."

Tamzea met my gaze with confusion. "What are you

talking about? Of course it was a poison. Mikla ran the tests to confirm it, and he—"

An image of all those rotting bodies flashed across my mind, the acrid scent of rot still clinging to me. "No. It was a virus manufactured by the Galvrarons for the Denards—but there was a double-cross and it's attacking humans. I—" Doubling over, I struggled to suck air into my lungs, my chest constricting to the point of pain.

"It was everywhere down there." I scrubbed at my arms. "Death. Death was everywhere. We could have brought it with us. It could be eating away at our insides as we speak." My vision wavered, and I swayed, strong arms wrapping around me in support.

"Shh … Neens, it's going to be okay. Do you hear me? We're safe. We just—"

"Mikla has to test you!" I screeched, searching for Maddox's face. But I couldn't find it amongst the wavering colors and spots dancing in front of my eyes. "Please, you could be dying right now. I won't lose you. Not now. Not after I just got you back."

"Put her over here. She's having a panic attack." Tamzea's voice was gentle and soothing. Not that it made a damn bit of difference to me. "I'll sedate her. We can't heal the mind. All we can do is make her as comfortable as possible until she calms down."

"She might shift," Maddox rumbled. "I've seen it happen with some of my team. She could rip the two of you to pieces before you knew what hit you, sedation or not. The wolf inside isn't easily controlled when panic takes over."

"Then we'll have to temporarily restrain her as well."

"What's she talking about with the virus? Is it founded in reality or is she having a complete meltdown?" Jane demanded, her voice going up a few octaves.

Thrashing against Maddox, I took a swipe through the air. "Calm down, Neens. Everything is going to be fine."

My arms and legs were tethered down, and something pricked the side of my neck. I roared my protest. "Please, Maddox needs tested. He's dying. He's dying right now. You have to save him!"

"As her mate, you can force her into a healing sleep," Xorik stated, his tone calm.

"Tell me how," Maddox commanded.

"You know how, simply allow your instincts to take over."

I thrashed against my bonds. "Something's not right. You all need to focus on Maddox, please! I can feel something is wrong with him." Something dark burned along the bond that connected us, eating away at what was left of my sanity. I had no proof, but I knew it was there. Maddox was sick … possibly dying.

"She's not wrong," Eron murmured. "His energies are going haywire."

A thump preceded a gasp, from Tamzea maybe. I blinked furiously, but I couldn't bring anything into focus.

"Fuck," Xorik muttered. "Look at his hand. It's like—"

"Get Mikla now," Jane commanded.

"We can heal it. Eron, help me," Tamzea said.

"Sleep, Nina." Xorik's hot breath touched my ear.

"No! I need to make sure Maddox is—"

"Sleep now."

Everything faded to black.

"MADDOX!" Eerie fog flowed around my feet, making it impossible to see where I was walking. "Maddox! Where are you?"

A hand reached up from the fog, latching onto my ankle. "Help me! You have to help me!"

I screamed. The hand wasn't much more than a bloody stump, and yet it somehow managed to cling to me. "Get off! Get off! Get off!" Kicking out, I connected with something solid, my boot pushing through the mass with ease.

I ran, moans of pain and pleas for help clogging my ears.

"Help me, I'm dying!"

"Please, save us!"

"You can't just leave us here!"

Suddenly Maddox was in front of me, half of his face rotted off. He smiled, flesh hanging limply from the one corner of his mouth. "Neens, baby, see … I told you I'd be fine." He staggered, dropping to his knees, his arm falling off. "Don't worry, it's just a flesh wound."

Scrambling to get to his side, I slipped, crashing to the

ground. Hands grabbed my arms and legs, pinning me spread eagle in place. "Let me go! I have to help him! I have to get to him! Please!"

Xorik's face swam before me. "Relax. Everything is under control. Maddox will be fine."

I shook my head. "No. No, did you see? He's dying. He's dying and I need to save him."

"You're having a nightmare, Nina. None of this is real."

"That's not true. We were on that planet." Shuddering, I remembered the corpses, the stench ... the green sludge. "The virus is going to kill us all."

"No. You'll be fine. And Maddox will be fine. Rest."

Screaming, I jolted awake, sweat covering me in a fine sheen. "Maddox," I croaked. "Where is he?"

"Stubborn to a fault," Xorik muttered. "I told you, Maddox is fine. Or he's going to be."

Lifting my head, I whipped it back and forth, realizing I was alone in the infirmary with Xorik. "How'd you get out of the cell, and where is everyone else?" I attempted to sit up but was stopped short by the restraints on my arms and legs. *What the hell?*

Xorik leaned back in the chair beside my cot, kicking his booted feet up. "Jane let me out. The second you started having your little meltdown she came to get me so I could help."

"Where's Maddox? Why isn't he here?"

Xorik smirked. "Like a damn broken record."

"What the hell is a record? And answer my questions, damnit!"

Xorik's eyebrows lifted. "I suppose my age is showing. Of course you don't know what a record is." He sighed.

"Where's Maddox?" I growled, my fangs shooting over my lower lip.

"You were right. He was infected, but don't worry. Mikla has already worked up an antidote … and some kind of barrier vaccine to prevent it from happening again."

Relief washed over me, and I sucked in a deep breath. "How long was I out?"

"A few hours."

"What about Jane? Was she infected, too?"

"No. Apparently, the whole fire thing within the phoenix DNA burns away the virus automatically. She's essentially immune. Which is why she and Ash went down to the planet to do some further investigating."

I nodded. "When can I see Maddox?" No matter what Xorik or anyone else said, until I laid my own eyes on Maddox, I wouldn't relax all the way.

Tamzea ambled into the room, Eron supporting her. "He's on the other side of the medical wing with Mikla. He's been sedated until …" She glanced at Eron, a silent conversation passing between them. "Well, he's going to be fine, but Dar is working on him now."

"Dar?" His expertise was within technology. He had no connection with medical procedures at all.

Ressi popped into existence beside me, curling into a ball at my side. "Don't worry, all of the most important parts are still there."

"What the hell are you talking about?"

Stretching out, she straightened her clothes. "Maddox. He just lost part of his arm. Nothing major."

My stomach twisted as I glanced at Tamzea and Eron. "What's she talking about?"

Tamzea stalked towards Ressi, waving her arms. "You need to shoo, get out of here. Shoo, shoo, shoo!"

Ressi hissed, her fur standing on end. "Hey! You can't just shoo me away like I'm a real cat. It's not my fault I was programmed to look like this. I was made to be appealing to a child!"

Ignoring her, Tamzea continued to wave her arms. "Shoo! I told you to shoo!"

Ressi glared at Tamzea. "I don't have to put up with this." She whizzed past her, her 3D image gliding into the hallway and disappearing.

"What was she talking about? And please," I strained my arms against my restraints, "can someone let me out of these? I'm not freaking out anymore so they're pointless."

Tamzea frowned, sitting on the edge of my cot. "I think, maybe, we'll tell you what she was talking about before we let you out of those."

My nostrils flared, and I sucked in a raspy breath. "What happened to Maddox? I thought you said he's going to be fine."

Tamzea's lavender gaze regarded me with sympathy. "And he is. He would have lost a lot more than part of his arm if Eron and I hadn't immediately started pouring healing energy into him. Between that and the antidote

Mikla gave him, the virus won't harm him anymore. But the damage is done."

"His arm? He lost his arm?" The virus must have started eating away at his flesh like it did to the Denards down on the red planet. "Was it painful?" What an idiot question, of course it was painful.

"Surprisingly, no," Eron interjected, his hands pressing into Tamzea's shoulders. "By the time any of us noticed what was going on, the virus had already eaten away at most of his hand."

"I need to see him."

Tamzea patted my leg. "Dar is working on him, which could take a few hours. Of course Masha is helping, too."

I ground my teeth together. "What are they doing to him that none of you seem to want me to witness?"

"Oh, for fuck's sake." Xorik stood, the chair clattering to the ground. "They're worried you're going to have another panic attack when you find out that Maddox is being fitted with a Gartian grade alloy prosthetic arm, much like the one Dar has himself."

I blinked, processing his words. "Maddox is going to be a cyborg? But how will that affect him when he shifts?" How the hell could a Lunin go wolfy if they had a mechanical arm made of Gartian-grade alloy? And where the hell had Dar tucked away the spare alloy? Not to mention the rest of the technology to make Maddox's transition possible? Did he travel with extra in case he needed repairs or was he simply paranoid?

Xorik scratched the stubble on his jaw. "I was

wondering the same thing myself about the shift, but Dar claimed to have a solution."

I swung my gaze up to Tamzea's again. "And why exactly am I not allowed to see him?"

"You need to let Dar and Masha concentrate. They don't need you as a distraction."

"Why is Dar helping? He hates me, and Maddox is my mate." Tamzea tilted her head, and I finally understood. "I can't go to Maddox while Dar is working on him because he doesn't want me there."

She nodded, her cheeks flushing. "Dar is helping Maddox, a New Earth military officer. He's an ally. He's not helping Maddox, the mate of a Denard, a hated enemy."

"And here I thought we were cool now."

Tamzea lifted lavender eyebrows. "Give him some time. Now you have some idea what his people went through … because of the Denards."

I bit my tongue, hating that she was right, but accepting it. I'd known the Denards had infected the Gartians with the G-Pox, but until I'd witnessed first-hand the rotting corpses on the red planet, I had no idea how horrible it must have been. I'd had no empathy—no true compassion. Now … now I knew. Or at least I could guess what it must have been like.

Maybe the Denards deserved nothing less than to be given a dose of their own hatred. Perhaps when it came down to it, it was merely karma delivering them the ultimate payback.

Chapter 29

I couldn't sleep. My anxious stomach combined with adrenaline was a no-doze cocktail that left me feeling a bit ill. Xorik had threatened to force me to sleep again, and Tamzea had brandished a syringe of sedative, but I'd threatened them both with bodily harm, which made them back off. Of course that meant I was still tethered to the damn cot in the infirmary, left to wonder what exactly was going on with Maddox.

"How much longer until I can go to him?" I hissed at Tamzea's back. She was organizing her supplies, something she seemed to do to keep herself busy when she was nervous.

Eron lifted his gaze to meet mine. He was lounging in the cot next to mine, his hands behind his head. "Masha will let us know."

"Does anyone know what Xorik is up to? I don't trust him."

Tamzea flashed a smile, shaking her head. "I pity the woman who takes him for a mate. He's a handful."

I snorted. "You mean pain in the ass."

She chuckled. "That too."

"So he really thinks he can just hop on over to New Earth and pick out a mate from the female Class 1s?" Eron asked.

I wiggled my legs and arms, unable to stay still. "I guess. Don't really care. I'm just happy he decided to leave me the hell alone on the mate front." Although I was secretly relieved for his changing bite. I wasn't sure how things would have worked with Maddox and me if I'd remained one hundred percent human, or if I'd even be alive. The virus had attacked Maddox aggressively, and he was only part human. Who knew what it would have done to me?

"Why didn't the virus infect me, too? Is it because I'm Lunin and not spliced?" I was almost one hundred percent positive that was the case, but I wanted to know for sure, especially if I needed to be careful in the future for some reason.

Tamzea closed the metal locker she'd been in. "Exactly. You are no longer human at all. You are Lunin. The virus will no more affect you than it will us."

"Are you sure? What if it mutates?"

Masha rushed into the room, her black eyes sweeping over me as a grin spread across her face. "We're done." With that she spun around, dashing back out the way she'd come.

Rocking from side to side, I flexed my arms and legs. "Let me up. You heard her. They're done. I need to see Maddox. Now."

Eron sprung to his feet, unlatching the bands quickly. I made grunting noises of impatience.

And then I was sprinting through The Pittsburgh, letting Maddox's scent be my guide.

"We'll be there shortly to check on him," Tamzea called after me, but I couldn't be bothered with a response.

Bursting into what appeared to be a makeshift lab, I skidded to a stop, my gaze alighting on Maddox who was lying in a bed, various tubes hooked up to his arms and legs.

In the corner of the room were Zula and Mikla, so caught up in a heated discussion, that neither of them noticed me.

"You knew this entire time. You knew Jane could be at risk and you didn't do anything," Zula hissed, her blue-tinged cheeks flushed to a lavender shade.

Mikla notched his chin up, eyes blazing with righteous indignation. "It would have been acceptable collateral damage. I—"

"Acceptable to who?" Zula shoved at him. "Jane is important to me. She's like a sister. Not that you would understand the true meaning of that evidenced by the way you treat me."

Scowling, Mikla stared at Zula's hands, as if he couldn't understand her violent tendencies. "Which is why you were never cut out to be a scientist. The

Galvraron council decided, although they would have preferred to avoid the death of New Earth-spliced humans, in order to rid the Universe of the Denards, it was an acceptable risk. One that we were hopefully prepared to counteract if the virus indeed did infect New Earth citizens."

"You played me for a fool with your feigned ignorance. I had no idea you could lie so well. And not every Denard deserves to die."

He shrugged, turning away from her. "Enough of them did that it made that an acceptable choice as well. And besides, it's not like I actually had a part in the production and distribution of the virus … and they were the ones who attacked our planet. They shouldn't have thought that brute force could outmaneuver a species such as ours."

Zula vibrated with fury. "You still could have said something—anything! By doing this the Galvrarons are just as bad as the Denards."

Trembling, my hand fluttered around my throat. "The Galvrarons actually did it? My mother said it was them—or you—but I never—I can't believe you knew!" Stalking towards Mikla, I jabbed my index finger at him. "You lied and said Maddox had been poisoned, and then you let us go down to that planet, knowing he'd already been infected once. What did you think was going to happen?"

"I thought that he'd probably built up an immunity to the virus since he'd already fallen ill from it once. As much as it pains me to say this … I was wrong. The Lunin DNA he was spliced with healed him completely, which in this case was a bad thing."

"Then why didn't the virus eat away at anything before? Why was it different in him the first time?"

Mikla rolled his eyes. "You really aren't that smart, are you?"

I smacked him across the face, barely keeping my rage in check. An indigo shaded handprint bloomed. "Just answer the damn question."

"Why is it creatures like you with subpar I.Q.s always resort to violence?" Rubbing his cheek, his scowl deepened. "Maddox must have been exposed to a watered-down form of the virus after it'd been carried around by other people."

"But where? Where did he come into contact with it? If it had been on Zeffrin then I would have been infected, too. Or if you two had brought it with you from your home planet," I stabbed my thumbs at myself, "again, I would have been infected. None of it—"

"Neens, baby, is that you for real this time?" Maddox rasped, drawing my attention away from Mikla.

Zula leaned into me, whispering, "He was delirious and kept thinking you were here, that everyone was you."

Rushing to his side, I climbed into bed with him, burying my nose against his neck. "It's okay. I'm here." I inhaled his scent, the gentle notes of cinnamon and dark chocolate comforting.

"What happened?" he groaned. "I don't understand how I keep ending up here."

I peered up at him from underneath my lashes. "Yeah, I'm over this whole visiting you in the medical wing thing. It was cute at first, but—" Two points of metal pinched my skin. "Ow, what the—"

"My hand feels strange," Maddox mumbled. "Not cold, but … cool, maybe … just weird."

He didn't realize part of his arm had been replaced yet. Sitting up, I reached for the metallic limb. It was attached just below his elbow, blending perfectly into his flesh.

I ran my hand over the smooth alloy, glancing at Maddox's face as I did. "What's that feel like?"

"Warm … and bizarre. What happened? Why are you blocking my view?"

Grimacing, I shuffled to my feet, letting him see what I'd been hiding. "Holy … fuck. I-I'm like Dar." He lifted his arm, flexing the mechanical fingers.

Mikla cleared his throat. "You're actually a very unique creature now. A doubly spliced human who is also a cyborg. You are the first of your kind." He straightened his lab coat. "You're welcome."

"What's with the tubes?" Maddox yanked on the one protruding from his left arm, the fingers of his right hand gleaming in the light as he moved them.

Shoving her brother aside, Zula met Maddox's dark gaze. "We wanted to make sure the antidote was evenly distributed throughout your body and reached everything at once to prevent any more rot from taking hold. Now the virus block is being filtered in so you'll be immune from now on."

"Block? You mean vaccine?" I asked.

Zula crossed her arms. "Yes, that's what I said … virus block."

I tapped one of the interpreter implants behind my ear. "Must be something lost in translation." Sometimes, although it didn't happen often, certain words did not translate well to my language. I wondered how often it happened with different species. No technology was infallible.

Jiggling the tubes again, Maddox scowled. "When can I get out of here? I need to get back to Zeffrin to check on everyone there, and then New Earth." Panic raced across his visage, tensing his jaw muscles. "What if the virus has already reached my people? What if—"

"Mikla is producing more of the antidote as we speak," Zula interjected. "We can deliver what we can to the scientists, and help them manufacture more there in their labs. But I won't lie … yes, there is a very real possibility that many are already dead or dying."

Mikla slumped into a chair, running his hands through his hair. "Yes, yes, I'll help the poor, mentally challenged, spliced humans because they can't figure out things for themselves." He ran a hand through his hair. "Have you ever heard of the Earth concept of Darwinism? Ironic how humans are the ones who should be eliminated according to that theory."

Zula kicked the chair out from under him, and he slammed to the ground, narrowly missing the corner of the desk with his temple. "Hey! If you injure me then there won't be any antidote or virus blocker."

Grabbing his arm, she yanked him to his feet. "Let's give them a few minutes to themselves," she growled, dragging him out of the room, his long legs tripping over themselves.

"I can't believe I'm a cyborg now." He shook his head slowly, his eyes transfixed to his metal limb. "These last few days—or has it been weeks—have been the weirdest of my life. I half expected to wake up back on my ship to find out none of it happened."

I threaded my fingers with his cool metal digits, a shiver running up my spine. "I hope it's not a dream because there were some pretty good parts along with the bad."

"I can't believe after everything, the Denards are gone."

I poked his stomach. "I mean us. That was the good part—us mating."

He grinned. "I know."

Settling into his side, I wrapped my arms around his middle. "Don't worry, I'm sure your people will be fine."

"I can't let myself think about it now or I'll go insane. We'll deal with whatever we find when we get to New Earth. There's nothing I can do from here." His heartbeat sped up. "I just hope there's a New Earth to save."

"You're right. As soon as Jane and Ash get back from the red planet, we'll be on our way, and there's no point in worrying about it until then."

As if on cue, Jane's voice crackled over the intercom.

"Listen up, everyone. We're going to be heading out in a few minutes, and as soon as we get going we're dropping directly into a light slide, so strap in and be prepared."

Mikla scuffled back into the room, his gaze averted. "I need to check to make sure my virus block is secured for the light slide."

"You never did say when Maddox could take out these tubes."

Mikla hummed under his breath, seemingly oblivious to the both of us as he fussed over various vials and tubes.

Heaving a long sigh of annoyance, I strapped Maddox and me to his bed.

Chapter 30

"Well, it appears that *all* the Denards weren't destroyed." Maddox scrubbed a hand down his face as he stared at The Pittsburgh's main computer screen over Zula's shoulder.

"How many UGFS ships are there?" I asked, my view obstructed by the back of Zula's head.

Her fingers flew over buttons, her brows scrunched in concentration. "Four from what our censors are picking up, but as you know, not all UGFS officials are Denards."

"No, just most of them," I offered.

"Okay, too many people in here." Jane shoved past Maddox and me, her expression thunderous.

"I thought you said that planet was the Denard stronghold?" Maddox's fingers dug into my arm. "What are they all doing here?"

I shook my head. "I don't know. I think it's pretty clear I'm not in the loop anymore, if I ever was."

"Five UGFS ships now," Zula muttered.

Standing on my tiptoes, I attempted to see over her head. We'd dropped out of a light slide near New Earth to find we weren't the only ones there for a visit.

"Try to hail New Earth again on the military channel," Maddox demanded. "We need to get down there."

Jane placed her hand on his shoulder. "Maybe it's better that we're not down there yet. I mean, I want to help, but I also want to live."

Maddox bared his teeth. "Jane, they're your people, too."

"And like I said, I want to help, but it's not going to do anyone any good if we die for nothing."

"A warrior's death is not nothing," Kade declared, his eyes glowing with a feverish gleam. Talsens were fighters, adhering to their own warrior code, which they were raised with from birth. It wasn't surprising that Kade wanted in on the action.

Zula glared at him over her shoulder. "Stop it with the warrior crap. We've talked about this. How would you feel if I—"

"Point taken." Kade scowled, his glowing irises dimming.

"Okay, seriously, there are too many people in here," Jane grumbled, flopping into her captain's chair.

Ash appeared beside her. "There's more than enough room, Jane."

She narrowed her eyes at him. "Spatially maybe, but not emotionally. I'm feeling crowded." She waved her arms over her head. "Everyone go back to where you were before we got here ... until I call for you."

"We're not leaving, Jane." Maddox's chocolate eyes sparked with gold. "You expect me to sit back and relax until you decide what's going to happen when that's my home planet down there!"

"I didn't say anything about relaxing." She adjusted a set of goggles in her hair, flames ghosting over her hands. "And it's my home planet, too. I don't want to see it get blown up!"

Maddox loomed over her. "You've never made it a secret about your Earth obsession. You don't consider New Earth your home planet, so quit the crap."

Jane jumped to her feet, flames running up her arms, and dancing in her eyes. Her lips curled back baring her teeth. "Don't you dare tell me what I do or don't care about."

Pressing in between them, I lifted my arms out. "I know tensions are high, but now is not the time to have petty arguments."

"Who's being petty?" Jane dropped her angry gaze to me. "You saying I'm being petty?"

"Want to shoot him in his arm again? This time it might bounce back and—"

"Enough!" Ash roared, his usually even tone reaching levels I didn't think possible. I covered my ears, and shook my head, cringing. "Now is not the time to turn on each other. Obviously, we need a plan." He plucked Jane off of her feet, disappearing in a cloud of smoke.

"Guess he told her," Tamzea said, her tone wavering. It was the first time she'd spoken in a while. I'd almost forgotten her and Eron were even in the room. It was clear she was a bundle of nerves. We all were, but she didn't hide her emotions well. Her skin was pallid, and her eyes twitchy. Eron leaned into her, whispering in her ear. Despite his efforts, she still wrung her hands together, her breathing shallow. Her obvious anxiety was ratcheting up mine.

I tugged on Maddox's arm, yanking him after me. "Come on, while Ash and Jane work up a realistic plan beyond just going down there with guns blazing, we can go check on Mikla and the vaccine."

He snorted. "Just go down there with guns blazing—when did I suggest that? It actually sounds like something Jane would come up with."

"Ash will manage her."

"And is that what you're doing with me now? Managing me?"

I smirked. "Maybe."

"Hmm," he grunted.

"What? You manage me sometimes, too. It's what happens in a relationship like ours. We take turns helping each other."

"So managing is helping?" Maddox wrapped his metal arm around me, tucking me into his side.

I shivered against the cool alloy. "How is your arm? Does it still feel weird?"

Lifting it away from his body, he stared at it, the

fingers flexing. "Yes ... and then no. It sucks that it's my dominant hand."

"I don't care what hand it is, as long as you're okay."

One side of his mouth curled up. "You might care later when my," he raised his hands to air quote, "cold hand finds its way to your more sensitive parts."

My brows furrowed. "Are you talking about during sex?"

"Of course I am."

Huh. I hadn't thought of that. Getting used to his new limb could be interesting. I hoped in a good way. Or at least that it wasn't weird somehow. "Really, your mind is on sex now?"

He shrugged. "It's the only thing that could potentially keep my mind off of what's going on out there right now."

Halting in the middle of the hallway, I stared at him. "Really?" Since my change, there was an almost constant hum of lust racing through my body. Not that I didn't think about sex before, but becoming a Lunin definitely upped my libido, that was for sure.

"I could probably help you with that."

His gaze heated as his fingers trailed through my hair. "Probably?"

"I mean, yeah, if I felt so inclined." Pressing into him, I nipped at his neck, eliciting a low rumble from him.

Dropping to his knees, he hitched my right leg over his shoulder, gazing up the line of my body. "Well, maybe I have a way that would incline you to help."

Grasping my pants, he ripped them right down the

middle, the cool air on my suddenly naked bottom causing goose bumps to erupt. "Maddox," I squeaked. "You just ripped my pants in half."

His eyes glimmered. "How else was I supposed to get to that sweet pussy of yours?"

"I don't know, maybe ask me to take—"

My words were stolen as his tongue slid along my clit, moving back and forth rapidly. Gone were any concerns for my pants, or for my nudity in the middle of the hallway. My entire focus narrowed down to Maddox's tongue and mouth, and the bundle of nerves he was laving his attention on.

"Were you saying something, Neens?"

"Maguallwaaah ..." Disconnected consonants and vowels tumbled from my lips, my brain unable to form coherent speech with Maddox between my thighs.

"That's what I thought," he growled against my flesh, redoubling his efforts.

His hands moved around to cup my ass, the cool metal of his right one holding me a bit too firmly, not that I cared in the moment. I writhed, both trying to escape and press closer to my tormenter.

"You—magic—tongue," I managed, right before I threw my head back, singing his praises to anyone with ears.

Still lost in ecstasy, I gasped in surprise when Maddox yanked me to the floor, covered me with his body, and plunged into me in one smooth thrust. I dug my claws into his shoulders, crying out.

"Fuck me harder. Please, Maddox, harder."

Pivoting against me, he complied, each thrust making stars dance behind my eyes, my body lost between pleasure and pain. Tumbling into another orgasm, I keened high, a sound eerily close to a howl.

Maddox's rhythm dropped away, his movements frantic as he pulsed his own release into me. "So fuckin' good," he muttered.

Falling on top of me, he was careful not to crush me with his body weight, instead supporting himself with just his right hand. "This thing is strong … stronger than that old piece of meat I had before. I might actually grow to like my new arm. And to think, I didn't even have the whole thing replaced. I'm holding myself up with just my fingers." With his free hand, he smoothed my sweat-dampened hair from my face. "Nothing like a quickie for a pick-me-up."

Footsteps sounded around the corridor, halting abruptly. "Great. Just great. Everywhere I go, all the beastly creatures are copulating. What's the point unless it's to procreate?"

I tipped my head back just in time to see Mikla storming away, his lab coat sweeping behind him dramatically. Pressing my face into Maddox's chest, I sniggered. "I don't think he's going to be happy to see us in a few minutes."

"He'll forget about it by the time we come back." Maddox disentangled himself from me and stood. Stooping to pick up my torn pants, he waved them in the air. "We might want to find you some new clothes before we pay Mikla a visit though."

My eyes narrowed in on Maddox's completely intact pants. "Why'd you go and rip mine? You could have simply asked me to take them off."

"It would have taken too long."

"But not yours? You—" He dipped down to sweep his tongue into my mouth. I blinked up at him. "Stop trying to shut me up with your magic tongue."

Chuckling, he trotted away. "Magic tongue."

"Hey! You get back here! I'm naked from the—"

A towel smacked me in the back of the head. I whirled around as Masha dashed off, a childlike giggle filling the air.

"What the hell?" I snatched the ratty towel, half of it covered with what I guessed was engine oil. Shrugging, I wrapped it around my waist, hurrying to find myself a new set of pants before Jane discovered me.

"Maddox!" I yelled. "You're a fucking asshole!" I couldn't believe he'd left me there, naked from the waist down. *I take back what I'd thought before about him sharing everything about himself with me. He can keep his playful side to himself sometimes. Especially if his sense of humor left me in potentially embarrassing situations.*

Chapter 31

"Oh, it's the rutting animals. How wonderful of you to visit me." Mikla's disdainful gaze slid from Maddox to me, and back again.

I elbowed Maddox in the ribs, hissing from the side of my mouth, "Not remember? Yeah, it absolutely seems like he doesn't remember to me."

"Well, what do you want? And if it's for me to leave my lab so you can copulate some more, the answer is no."

"We wanted to check on your progress with the antidote and vaccine production," I mumbled.

"I'm right where I should be as far as the timeline goes because I've been here in this lab, working steadily, not running around the ship half naked and—"

"Yeah, we get it … copulating," Maddox snapped. "But it's not as if any female would be excited to get it on with you anyway."

"Maddox," I hissed. "Not nice." Not that I particularly

cared about the insult in itself, but antagonizing the scientist who was going to be providing vital services didn't seem like the wisest idea.

Maddox shrugged, completely unrepentant. "What? It's true."

Mikla's blue cheeks heated, turning them a solid shade of lavender. "Plenty of Galvraron females were interested," he waved his hand in our direction, "in doing that with me."

"Really?" Maddox guffawed. "How many—"

I elbowed Maddox again. *Seems like the sexual distraction worked a little too well. He doesn't seem to want to deal with anything serious at all.* "No one cares. Tell us about the vaccines and antidotes."

Mikla straightened his lab coat, fidgeting from foot to foot. "Like I said, I'm right on schedule. The first batches are complete. Although both the antidote and virus block may need to be adjusted since I'm basing them off of Maddox's genetic makeup, and he is doubly spliced."

"What? But I thought the Galvrarons had a backup plan or protocol if something went wrong with the virus and it attacked spliced humans along with the Denards. That's what you said." I turned to Maddox. "Isn't that what he said?"

Mikla sniffed. "We did have something ready … on our planet. But the brain matter deficient Denards went and attacked us."

A deep growl rumbled within Maddox's chest, and fangs shot out from his gums. "We have to save the citizens of New Earth." His gaze was wild, panicked almost, and yet somehow still focused.

Okay. So he wasn't acting worried because he thought it was taken care of, or would be as soon as we could get down to the planet. I brushed my palm down his arm, drawing his attention. "You being angry isn't going to change anything. We'll do the best we can, that's all anyone can ask for."

Shirking out from under my touch, he slammed his fist into the wall, leaving an impressive dent. "Our best doesn't matter if it isn't good enough." He stalked from the room, snarling under his breath.

"Maddox, wait!" I rushed after him.

Jane grabbed my arm, seemingly having appeared out of nowhere. I flailed, teetering on my heels. "Let him go. He's always been a bit of a brooder. Annoying, if you ask me."

"He has every right to be—"

"You're coming with me, so you're just going to have to worry about him later." She tugged me along, her strength considerably more than mine even with my new Lunin DNA.

"Where?" I gritted out, dragging my feet along the floor, getting absolutely no traction on the smooth metal.

"To one of those UGFS ships. They've been sitting there, doing nothing, and we need to know why."

"What do you expect them to do? Send out a detailed plan over all the comms?"

"Ha! You think you're funny, don't you? But I'm being

serious here. They haven't so much as flickered a light. Something isn't right and we need to find out what it is."

"And why am I your choice for a companion?"

She lifted her brows. "Haven't we been over this? Duh, Denard … even if you aren't anymore, you sure fooled them before, so if the plan isn't broken then let's not try to fix it."

I scrunched up my nose. "The saying doesn't go like that, it—"

"Don't care," she snapped.

We arrived at the airlock, Zula and Ash hushing their conversation as soon as we were in earshot. Jane scowled. "I better not find out that you two are talking about me behind my back again. I thought I told you that if you care about someone you talk shit to that someone's face."

I snorted. It was such a Jane thing to say. "So does that mean you like me?"

Jane dropped my arm. "Don't get ahead of yourself. I don't not like you. It's about all you can hope for at the moment after all the crap you pulled."

I grinned, shaking my head. "Okay, whatever you say."

"All right, here's the plan." Jane yanked on a spacesuit, kicking one at me. "We're going to sneak onto the closest UGFS ship and have a look around."

Ash rolled his eyes. "Doesn't sound like much of a plan to me. How are you even going to get into a ship like that?"

"I'll figure it out," she huffed, pulling the helmet over her head.

Ash rapped on the front, his knuckles pinging against the plastic. "Why are you still wearing one of these? You know you don't need it."

She slapped his hands away. "Don't start with me about this stuff when you won't help me more with my fire form."

An arm wrapped around my waist, tugging me backwards. Hot breath fanned along the nape of my neck, bringing with it Maddox's unique scent. "Weren't you even going to say good-bye?"

Spinning within his grip, I gazed up at him. "What's the point? I would have been right back."

"Never take anything for granted." His lips brushed against mine, soft at first before taking on an edge of desperation.

"Okay, love birds," Jane snarked, "break it up before I have to throw water on you."

Pulling away from Maddox, I drank him in with my eyes before spinning around to pick up the space suit. I made quick work of putting it on and snapped the helmet into place.

"I'm ready."

"About time," Jane muttered, her voice coming from the speaker in my helmet.

"UMM ... I thought you said you'd figure out a way in?"

Jane and me were hanging outside a UGFS cruiser ...

literally. And we'd been there for at least ten minutes without any signs of things changing.

"Shut up. I'm trying to think."

"Why don't you burn a hole in one of the maintenance entranceways?" I spun around to face The Pittsburgh, my back plastered against the cruiser. Could Maddox see me? Was he worried? Was he even watching? There was nothing ...well, except everything to be scared of. "We need to get the hell in the ship or go back. I can't turn into flame like some people and if I get sucked out into space I'm screwed."

"You're not going to get sucked out into space," Jane scoffed. "I mean, how many times have you heard of that actually happening to someone?"

"More times than I can count."

"Oh. Really? Huh."

"That's it. I'm going back." I reached for the tiny cord connecting us.

"Fine. Fine. I'll burn a way into one of the maintenance entranceways. Happen to know where any of them are?"

"Oh, for fuck's sake." I twisted the knob on my thrusters, releasing some of the pressure that was keeping me up against the ship, and bounded carefully across the top. "There's usually one along here somewhere in most UGFS cruisers."

"See, this is one of the reasons I brought you along."

"There." I motioned to a small hatch several feet in front of us. "Do your thing before I find myself admiring the scenery as I float off into it."

Jane bounded ahead of me, and I twisted around so our cord wouldn't get tangled. She dropped to her knees, flames shooting out of her palms, and burning the material covering her hands. She gasped, her face panicked, before she burst into flames. Floundering, I scrambled to disconnect our cord before the fire made its way to me and burnt me to a crisp.

She passed right into the hatch, flinging it open a second later. Jumping for it, I arced high before adjusting my thrusters. I flew down the small shaft, landing in a heap at the bottom of a ladder as soon as the artificial gravity grabbed hold of me.

Jane slammed the hatch closed, standing over me in smoldering and tattered clothes, her space suit gone. "Sorry about that. I thought I could manifest the flames outside of my suit but I apparently can't do stuff like that yet."

Yanking off my helmet, I shimmied out of my space suit, letting it drop to the ground. "You should have listened to Ash and just come over in your flame form to begin with so you wouldn't put me in danger."

She raised her hands. "It all worked out in the end so stop complaining. You're just as bad as Zula and Tamzea."

Lumbering to my feet, I glared at her. "Have you stopped to consider that maybe it's not all of us? That you're the problem?"

She waved me off, dropping to her knees to crawl into the tunnel in front of us. It was a dismissal. Of course, she'd never consider the fact that she was the problem—reckless and out of control as she was.

"Don't leave that suit behind. They're expensive."

Like hell I'm going to drag it around with me. I knew where I left it and either I'd steal a new one or I'd come back for it. Grinding my teeth together, I dropped down to enter the tunnel myself. It was dark, but I managed to see clearly with my improved Lunin night vision. As I crawled along behind Jane, I wondered what other nifty upgrades I'd find as time went on. And the Denards thought getting spliced was bad. I snorted. Fear had stifled them in so many ways. I couldn't begin to fathom what they'd missed out on over the centuries.

"Looks like this ride is about to end," Jane whispered. "Be ready for … whatever."

What we were doing was beyond asinine if you asked me, obviously Jane hadn't. What good was sneaking onto the ship really going to do? There was no way we were going to go completely unnoticed. We'd be lucky if we weren't greeted by half a dozen laser guns being shoved in our faces at the end of the tunnel. *Please don't let me get killed on this stupid ship going along with Jane's ridiculous non-plan plan.*

"Stop right where you are," Jane commanded. "You smell that?"

Lifting my head to sniff the air, the pungent aroma of death and decay slammed into me, causing me to gag.

"I'll take that retching sound as a yes. You stay here. I'm going to zoom around the ship in my flame form. I have a feeling we both know what we're going to find, and there's no point in you having to see it again."

She shifted into flame, racing off, leaving a trail of smoke in her wake. Covering my nose and mouth with my arm, I scuttled backwards awkwardly, wanting to put as much distance between the virus and me. *It's here. I can smell it.*

"What's wrong?" Maddox's voice swam through my mind.

Despite everything I found my lips twitching up. He was communicating with ease telepathically. It was wondrous. "Jane's checking things out. But I think all these people are dead."

"The virus."

"Yes. I can scent it now. It has a—"

"Yeah, a sickly-sweet odor. I'd recognize it now, too."

I nodded, even though he couldn't see me. "Jane wants me to wait here, but I think I need to check the ship out, to find out if I can pull any transmissions or information from the database—"

"Um, hello? That's what I'm here for." Ressi danced around in the small space in front of me, her tail twitching with excitement. "I'll be back in a second." She flew off in the same direction Jane had gone.

"Guess I won't have to," I communicated to Maddox. "We'll be back soon."

Panting into my arm, I continued to backtrack to where I'd left the space suit, eager to escape the noxious odor permeating my senses. Funny how I hadn't noticed it right away, but once I did, I couldn't seem to smell anything else.

"Love you, Neens. Meet me on New Earth." And with that, Maddox shut down the mental connection between us, his abrupt exit jarring.

New Earth? Yeah, if Maddox thought everyone on the UGFS ships were dead, the first thing he'd do was hightail it down to New Earth. Hopefully, what we found there would be better than what we found on this ship.

Epilogue

We'd been waiting around since the Denard attacks for something to happen, and then the virus had … and things escalated quickly.

It had been the silent marauder let in the back door to obliterate all the Universe thought it knew.

Denards weren't some mysterious alien species, but a faction of pureblooded humans simply hiding under a different name. The UGFS wasn't maintaining peace, concerned for the welfare of all of those under its jurisdiction, but a group of politicians, human and other, using it as a guise to further its own agendas.

The secrets were out, and no one knew who to trust anymore. Although it was clear that some kind of government needed to take control. The UGFS hadn't been a bad idea, merely one that had fallen into the wrong hands. As they say … Power corrupts, and absolute power corrupts absolutely. Of course, that saying aptly was born on Earth, humans always seeming to have been the biggest offenders.

Although the Galvrarons were the ones who created the virus, no one seemed to hold them culpable, especially after the atrocities the Denards had committed over the years. And even though some innocent casualties were amassed among New Earth citizens, the antidote was administered, and all seemed to want to move towards the future.

We didn't live in the type of Universe where dwelling in the past did much good, the sudden end of the Denards a prime example of what happened when revenge and fear motivated a species. Not to say that humans had been completely eradicated—the few who managed to survive became other things … whether it was a Lunin or a spliced citizen of New Earth, many options existed for a pureblooded human looking to become more than they thought they could ever be.

In a way, a new species was born, all of us different, yet our origins tracing back to one place: Earth. We were conceived in something beyond what the Denards would have ever comprehended—we were formed out of tolerance instead of hate, and maybe one day that would grow to true understanding, although it was difficult to predict such things. In the end, all it had taken was the true threat of extinction, and under such dire circumstances, apparently even humans could be forced to change.

As for the rest of the Universe …

Would true peace ever exist?

Well, everything is temporary, nothing ever remaining in stasis. As long as there are differences between people and species there will be hate and fear. It was an unfortunate truth. The best one could hope for is indifference instead of malice. You can't ignore someone to death, after all.

"So which one will it be?" Maddox asked, shaking me from my reverie. "Go or stay?"

"Whichever you want. Doesn't really matter to me as long as we're together."

"I don't know how much time I can spend with Jane, honestly. That woman drives me insane. But I know you've become rather fond of the crew on The Pittsburgh."

"We both need to be happy." Rolling over, I wrapped my arms around Maddox's middle, pressing my face into his back. He was sitting up on the edge of our bed, chin perched on his intertwined hands. "Just because I like them doesn't—"

"And I like them, too!" Ressi exploded into existence in front of Maddox, glaring at him. "Don't make us suffer because you're still upset that Jane shot you in the arm twenty-some years ago! How big of a broody baby are you?"

Maddox glanced at me over his shoulder. "I thought we talked about her hanging around all the time. It's creepy."

"I'll give you creepy, you big, old—"

"Ressi, we did talk about this. I won't look into finding you more upgrades like the ones you wanted if you don't—"

She disappeared, obviously not wanting to risk her upgrades.

Shifting, I pulled myself up, leaning my head on Maddox's shoulder. "Now that your service is over with the military, we can do whatever we want. We don't have to choose between going to The Pittsburgh or settling down on New Earth. We can do both, or neither, the possibilities are endless."

He spun, swooping me up in his arms. I giggled as he peppered kisses along my face as he spoke. "It's utter chaos out there right now in the Universe, and I have no idea when things are going to settle down again. I don't want to be putting you in constant danger."

"So maybe you take that position as a diplomat of New Earth, and help iron out some of that chaos? I know you're not one for politics, but—"

"We'll talk about his later. Right now, I can't think straight with you being naked and in my arms."

I moaned when he pressed into me, the weight of his body pinning me to the bed.

Yeah, sure, I can get on board with whatever he wants, as long as he never lets me walk out of his life again.

The End? Or just the beginning … ?

Acknowledgments

As an overthinker, acknowledgments are quite an arduous task for me. I wonder if I'm being lackluster or too intense with the thanks. Or did I forget someone? Possibly I gave too much credit to someone and therefore slighted someone else who actually did a ton. A part of me doesn't want to include these in my books at all because the people I appreciate should know it already … or do they??? No matter how I look at it these damn acknowledgments make me friggin' sweat.

But here they are anyways since if I don't include them then people will probably think I'm ungrateful and weird. I mean, I am weird, but I don't want people to think that. I am grateful though, so I'll just go-ahead and make this uncomfortable for everyone. Heh.

Okay, here I go. Right now. Actual acknowledgments to follow. Hopefully, they represent an appropriate level of gratitude to all the people in my life that deserve it.

(And yep … I have totally copy & pasted what comes next from my *Replayed* book acknowledgments, which I originally took from *Virtual Reality Bites* acknowledgments. I thought maybe after *Replayed* that I'd come up with something better. Or at least something new. Obviously not. So this is now copy & paste edition #6. Or 7? 8? Who even knows anymore. Therefore, I'm thinking you should probably get used to it.)

My amazing Hubby! Words can't begin to explain how supportive and truly amazing he is. Hmmm … I think I already used the word amazing. But unlike in books, when honestly applied to someone, the word amazing means something, well, amazing. And my hubby is all of the things that word implies. Romance heroes are nothing compared to him.

Lindsay Tiry … what would I do without you? I hope I never have to find out. From cover design to interior graphics to logos, you do it all. Your talent is awe-inspiring, and I hope one day everyone else will be able to appreciate how you shine.

Melissa Ringsted … my illustrious editor. Without you, this book probably would have gone straight into the trash. Thank you for giving me the confidence to publish when I convinced myself that I was the worst writer in the history of writers, and for fixing all the words.

Ren, Kristin, Shona, Ruty … my O.G. chicas … I wouldn't be here without you. I'm beyond lucky to know all of you.

And last, but certainly not least, thank you to everyone who has taken the time to read this book. Hopefully, you enjoyed it, but even if you didn't, I still appreciate the fact that with so many options out there today, you even gave my book a fleeting chance.

About the Author

Ava Wixx escaped into books at a young age and decided to stay there. It was only a matter of time before she was driven to create her own fantasy worlds from fear of running out of places to explore.

Reader, writer, dreamer … Ava only toils in reality when absolutely necessary. She lives in North Carolina with her husband, and spoiled mini-poodle.

www.ingramcontent.com/pod-product-compliance
Lightning Source LLC
LaVergne TN
LVHW091108080826
845145LV00008B/1843

* 9 7 8 1 9 5 5 9 5 0 2 7 5 *